14 Shorts & Other Dirty Laundry

Joel Reiff

14 Shorts and Other Dirty Laundry

The Laundry List:

After Shock

"Do you want to know when you will die?"

Julian Tavares sat back until his gaze was almost even with the crystal ball spanning the distance between him and the fortuneteller. Everything about The Great Renaldo was decrepit, from the cigarette-stained hands and thinning gray hair to the dreary trailer they sat in. There were no astrological charts or magical talismans adorning the walls. No oversized Tarot deck spread out over the table boasting medieval pictures of devils and knights. The Great Renaldo was of a different pedigree from the frauds at the circus and county fairs that had the look but not the sight. Or so his research had revealed. Staring at the dull, lidded eyes of the man, he wondered if this soothsayer could foresee what would happen if he decided to betray his best friend?

"The man that pulls the trigger does not necessarily point the gun," the old man said.

Julian leaned forward far enough for his exhale to briefly fog the crystal ball. "Look, Renaldo. I drove a good hour to get here. I'm not one of those housewives that want to know if love or prosperity is around the corner or some loser looking to fall in love or get rich quick."

The corners of Renaldo's mouth curdled upwards in a poor excuse for a smile. "Words. They play together like children. And children can be so cruel to one another."

Julian pushed the rickety table back and stood up. "Why the hell did I even bother," he said more to himself than to the fortuneteller.

"You bothered because your friend Clarence Digby told you that I predicted his heart attack to the very day." Renaldo leaned back and clasped his hands over his small belly. "You have not slammed the door behind you because an associate of yours told you about my prediction of the recent market crash. To the day."

Julian looked at the empty pizza box near the trailer's small sink. Clothing that wouldn't be accepted by the Salvation Army lounged on the ratty miniature sofa pushed against the wall. If this man knew so much important information, why did he live in such squalor?

4

"I know that look," Renaldo said. "It is similar to the one you often give your friend, Anders."

Julian felt weakness overtake him life a virus. He hadn't mentioned Anders to this man. Without averting his eyes, he slowly sat back down and placed his hands back on the table. "Tell me when I will die."

Renaldo's gnarled fingers opened to receive payment. Julian leaned forward and placed the wad of cash in the man's hand, which closed mechanically around the bills.

"You will die in thirteen days."

Julian's face remained placid. Thirteen days. Three-hundred-and-twelve hours. Eighteen thousand, seven hundred and twenty minutes. What was left of a life. "What is it you people have with the number 'thirteen'?"

"Thirteen is only lucky or unlucky depending on your beliefs. Judas was the thirteenth participant at the Last Supper, which was bad luck for Christ, no? There are thirteen lunations in a year. According to the Torah, God has thirteen Attributes of Mercy. The sacred cord of Druids has thirteen segments.

"I am not a Jew or a Druid."

"No, you are a Sikh, are you not?"

"Does my skin tone reveal so much to you or does your crystal ball do racial profiling?"

"Julian is not your given name. Not exactly Sikh, is it?"

"Let's not talk 'stage' names, okay? Renaldo?"

Renaldo swallowed the insult with his pride, a combination often made palatable when one is paid more for what he withholds then reveals. With a knowing smile, he covered the crystal ball with a purple velvet cloth.

A small hole in the fabric made the glass appear to glare at Julian. If the ball represented his entire life, was that tiny circle all that was left?

"In Sikhism," Renaldo said, "the number thirteen means 'yours,' as in of the Lord's. You may take that as either a sign, a coincidence, or the spiritual prattling of a wise man."

Julian's first thought was disbelief. Thirteen days? He was thirty-seven years old and hadn't taken a sick day in over ten years. Ridiculous. This was just a well-played sham. A party joke without a punch line. What kind of fortune teller blurted out such nonsense without any pretense? Or any warning? These types always played up the drama. No, this Great Renaldo was a kook, and he a fool and a sucker. When he rose, the force of his body sent the chair toppling over. "You are not that wise."

"As you wish."

"Have you spoken to Anders?"

"I have had no contact with your business partner whom you refer to as your best friend."

5

Julian didn't know whether to smack the man or press him for an explanation. He didn't recall if he had mentioned Anders since he arrived. And certainly wouldn't tell anyone he was his best friend. Especially not Anders. He stared hard at the charlatan before him, bit down hard, and left without another word. To make The Great Renaldo into The Late Renaldo would be a lapse in judgment. Other people made those.

On the ride home, he cursed himself for falling prey to superstition. The Great Renaldo could have unearthed those nuggets of information about him and his associate Anders with a laptop and Internet access. Still, the man had been spot on about Digby's double bypass. As he approached the outskirts of Houston, he thought of a second question he should have asked the old fortune-teller, one that may have been more enlightening: "*How* will I die?"

*   *   *

Julian nudged Evangelina's side. She ignored him and continued to read her book in bed. He looked at his wife and felt great pride. Even though she'd put on a few pounds while he remained svelte, he found her to be a stunning woman. The type people were jealous of when he escorted her into a highfaluting Wall Street fete or the private party of some major investor. His pleasure came from watching the eyes of her admirers rather than her own expressions. He nudged her again.

"Stop," she said with a lack of playfulness only a marriage could endure.

"What are you reading?" he asked.

Evangelina let out a defeated sigh. She methodically extracted her bookmark from the last page and placed it inside the book, closed it and laid it on her lap with her hands collapsed over it. "It's the Vampire Trilogy. You know, the one you gave me for my birthday via gift certificate?"

After twelve years of marriage he had lost track of what he gave her and when he gave it. Jewelry, clothing, and international travel filled her time while he toiled away locking in investors. As an aspiring artist, he'd always provided her with any experience she needed. Hard to imagine a woman needing anything more in her life.

"I thought you were reading that coffee table book I gave you. What was it? *Three Hundred Years of Art*, or something?"

She gave him a look of disbelief. "It was called *30,000 Years of Art*, and that was nearly two years ago."

"Oh." He slid his body closer to hers and placed a tentative hand on her breast. "Hey, Ev, I'm feeling a little randy tonight."

Suppressing a groan, she turned to look at him with anything but desire. Her lids half closed and her brown hair framed her face. Wrinkles threatened the perfection of her chocolate skin. "Why don't you forward me a request via Blackberry and I can have your secretary schedule a date and time so that we both will know when it should happen?"

He removed his hand. "Is it that time of the month?"

She huffed at his comment. "Passion isn't a switch. I haven't even seen you for the past two weeks."

She always had some lame excuse lately. He moved back over to his side of the bed and lay on his back with his hands flat on his taut stomach. She shook her head once and resumed her reading.

After a few, turgid moments he asked, "How is the new piece coming along?"

She closed her eyes for a count of ten. Closing her book with finality, she placed it on the nightstand and turned out the light. She lay down with her back facing him. "Why do you ask questions when you either know the answer or don't care what it is?"

"When did it become a crime to try and engage my wife in a conversation?" he said.

"I'm sorry," she said perfunctorily and without remorse. "I'm very tired. If you must know, the latest piece has been giving me trouble."

There once was a time when she confided in him about what she was working on. Even asked his opinion, despite his never having one. Art wasn't logical. In finance, although you worked the numbers to their greatest advantage, two plus two always equaled four. Colors and shapes didn't add up the same way each time and value was completely subjective.

"I'm supposed to die in thirteen days," he said.

She didn't answer.

"Did you hear what I said?"

She turned halfway. "Can we talk about this tomorrow?"

He rolled out of bed and turned out his nightstand light. As he stared into the darkness with his back to his already snoring wife, he thought about Renaldo's words and kicked himself for even mentioning it. Ev didn't take it seriously; why should he? He got back into bed and closed his eyes, but his mind wouldn't let it go. When it became obvious that sleep was not on the agenda, he got up and quietly put on his slippers for a foray into the den. Two glasses of brandy helped if not to soften his mood, then his mind. Even while a little inebriated, he couldn't stop thinking about Renaldo's prediction.

He wakened his computer and scanned the recent headlines that had been dogging him. Anything to divert his thoughts from his own mortality. The Securities Exchange Commission was cracking down on questionable business practices and he was currently in their sights. Two major banks had called their loan markers and he didn't have the cash flow to cover them. His investors were inundating him with texts and emails while his potential bailout clients had stop taking his. In short, he was backed to the edge of the precipice. Add the economy bottoming out and someone had to pay the piper. With interest.

The third glass of brandy seemed wasteful, so he left it on the table and wandered to the basement studio he'd fashioned for Evangelina. It had all the accouterments an artist could want. Canvases, some finished and others half-conceived, leaned against walls or sat in racks. She had an astounding supply of paints. Colors with designer names like Mars Violet and Phtahalo Green. He used to imagine that the countless hues were like the nuanced feelings his wife had for him. Lately, it seemed she'd gone monochromatic.

The canvas on her easel seemed to corroborate his theory. She'd always painted in colorful abstracts. This current work was mostly brown, blood red, and black. Two hangman-like stick figures in thick brush strokes were on one side of a swirling red whirlpool, seemingly trying to resist the vortex's pull. A black figure in the center, half the size of the other two, seemed to suck them under. Towards the top was a harsh line of black, and a forbidding 'sky' of red.

He leaned forward until his face was right next to the canvas. The smell of acrylic filled his nostrils. He stepped back to take in the entire image. What was it she was trying to say? Artistic 'symbolism' was never his forte. The painting brought chaos to mind. As a man who thrived on order, the overall feeling was distasteful.

Chaos. Yes, that would be how he'd dodge this SEC bullet aimed at his wallet. He decided right then that Anders had to take the fall for what they had done.

* * *

Anders Delarosa was a diminutive man. The kind you could never recall being around, but always ended up in the picture. An unremarkable face and an even more unremarkable presence. What he lacked in physical stature, he made up for in mental capacity. Julian had never known a sharper, faster-thinking individual. He could out-process a calculator, out-project an analyst armed with a week's worth of economic charts, and out-maneuver the most adept financial minds. His single-minded attention to detail regarding the task at hand left him oblivious to cataclysmic happenings around him. When the Twin Towers went down his business partner didn't notice the bedlam in the office as everyone scrambled to leave; the man had some numbers that were more important and engaging. Julian would use this lack of peripheral vision to frame him for all of their current troubles.

"We must hold off our creditors for at least another ten days," Julian said, trying to look as concerned as his words implied. Three days ago The Great Renaldo had given him thirteen days to live. All his life he'd given fate a firm middle finger, and now was no time to change his style.

Anders' nose nearly touched the computer he was typing on. Just out of his reach was Thursday's Wall Street journal with a headline decrying the fraudulent dealings of businesses such as theirs. He took another slurp of coffee and set the cup down on the newspaper.

"My projections don't tell a very pretty picture," Anders said, scratching his nose with a pencil. "I don't see how we can hide these delinquent debts any longer. We'd need some creative accounting that would make the guys at Enron blush." He shook his head back and forth before looking up at Julian. "What do you propose we do?"

Julian walked away from his partner in crime and faced the window. Three stories below, people walked along Lamar Street in the afternoon heat. "We can salvage this situation," he said to his reflection in the glass.

"How do you propose we do that?"

Julian turned to look at his partner. "You release a statement that you stand by both our investors and investments. Talk up how our projected returns are attainable based on last year's third quarter earnings. Take the heat off of me by taking responsibility for any misconceptions the SEC may have. Do it tomorrow, a Friday. That way, it won't be headline news until Monday. That'll give me the weekend to nail down solid backup investors without the SEC on my back. Monday afternoon I'll shift the blame from both of us by claiming I was duped into making these investments and had no knowledge of the questionable accounting these companies are exhibiting."

Anders was silent a moment. "That leaves me vulnerable."

"Only for the weekend. Which you will spend out of town. I have your ticket and hotel reservation for a brief visit to Puerto Vallarta right here." Julian patted his breast pocket.

"You always make those trips," he said. "What will I do there by myself?"

Ah, poor Anders. With the money they'd both made, he could have just about any woman. The only figures he wrapped his hands around were the ones on his beloved balance sheets and financial projections that kept him working well past when Julian left for a posh dinner or two-hour massage.

"Pack an overnight bag with just the essentials." Julian spread his arm to encompass the avalanche of paper spread before the man. "Leave all this behind. Enjoy yourself for once."

Anders looked unsure. "I've wanted to go to Mexico for years."

"About time you did." Julian knew Anders lived vicariously through him. By putting him on that plane to Mexico, Anders could pretend, for just one weekend, that he *was* him.

"It sounds great."

"It will be great. Just don't drink too much tequila."

Julian forced a smile that Anders returned. The month being June, the man had no idea that the Mexican rainy season could start at any time. What he knew for sure was that the SEC storm wouldn't end after the weekend for his soon-to-be-former partner.

*   *   *

Friday the thirteenth came and went without incident. Julian had eight more days, according to The Great Renaldo. Eight had always been his lucky number. Smiling faces of the children he'd sponsored from Azerbajian to Zimbabwe graced his office wall from the $800,000 he'd donated to worthy causes. He'd just celebrated his eighth year of marriage to Evangelina, having tied the knot on Aug. 8. Still, his sleep never seemed deep and he awoke at the slightest noise from the construction crew on the street. There would be no sympathy from his wife. She was locked away in her studio.

He phoned a business associate and arranged a lunch meeting. Checking his watch, he figured that Anders would be facing the press any minute before junketing off to Mexico. Best to be seen in public when the shit hit the fan.

Over a blackened tilapia sandwich and side salad he traded stories will Bill Naswell, a trader he'd worked with before all of his success and accompanying hassles. Bill was a straight arrow, a man who wouldn't even jaywalk. Being in his company at a posh downtown restaurant couldn't hurt his street cred. The waitress cleared away their plates and dropped off a desert menu when Bill dropped the bomb.

"Did you hear about Carlson from the SEC?"

"No, what about him?" Carlson was one of the agents on his case. Of all of the wolves out to get him, Carlson was the only one who seemed to be open to his innocence. The only one who didn't want to nail him to the cross and grab the headlines.

"Got hit by a stray bullet while buying ice cream with his kids right on his own street. Seems some kids were messing with their mother's gun on the front lawn and the thing had a round in the chamber."

"That's terrible. Talk about a...freak accident."

"That isn't even the freaky part. I date his secretary, this hot brunette named Rita. She does this thing with her tongue–"

"Tell me about the Carlson freaky part, not the Rita freaky part."

"Oh...yeah...she told me that he'd been to a fortune teller out in the desert a couple of weeks earlier. She found the dude for him. The Great Gonzo or something like that."

Renaldo, Julian wanted to correct him.

"She's way into all of that tarot card crap. Stars in alignment, energy fields, all kinds of wacked out stuff. But, she's got great tits."

"Carlson." The two tables next to theirs stopped conversation and looked over at them. He ducked his head and lowered his voice. "You were telling me about the fortune teller he saw."

"Yeah, some washed up fortune teller in an old trailer out in the desert. Tells Carlson that he has lived on numbers with wings and that these numbers will, and I quote here, 'take flight against him and he will die by a child's hand'. There was also something in there about the ice cream truck."

Julian didn't wait for the waiter to bring the check. He dropped a fifty on the table and rushed to his car. The speedometer pushed ninety mph on the drive out of town. In another ninety minutes he'd arrive at the trailer of the Great Renaldo. Perhaps if he knew how he was going to die, he could avoid it. This was all too weird. He wanted answers.

Renaldo's lair broiled in the sun on a dirt road five miles off the highway. When he knocked on the screen door precariously hanging by one hinge, no one answered. After a second failed attempt, he tried the door. The latch must have been broken because all he had to do was push. The trailer looked as decrepit as when he last visited. Large cockroaches munched on crumbs in the pizza boxes by the sink. They didn't bother to scatter when he walked in on their feast. The flimsy card table sat in the middle of the cluttered room. A few days' dust accumulated on the crystal ball waiting patiently in the center. A note attached to the top was addressed to 'Mr. Julian Tavares' written in a shaky hand.

He recoiled before reaching a tentative hand towards the note. He cast a glance around the cramped room. "Renaldo?" Dead quiet. The slap of a stick or tumbleweed against the side of the trailer made his heart skip a beat. He went outside, but no one was around. Heat rippled the horizon. This time when he walked back inside, the roaches abandoned their meal and scattered out of sight.

11

The note stared back at him. He reached out to grab it, being as careful as if it were a snake that might rear back and strike at any moment. Dust swirled as he detached the note from the glass ball. His heart pounded as he opened the lined piece of paper. The same scribbled writing inside read, 'No one can protect you from yourself.'

*   *   *

That evening Justin watched the news alone in his study. The analysts and pundits on the Business channels spewed out enough dirt to fill the grave Anders had dug for himself. The Mexico trip only made his guilt look more plausible. When his partner got back he would be arrested immediately. He felt a pang of regret at having thrown the poor man to the wolves, but he found solace in the knowledge that all was going according to plan.

The news services called it a Ponzi scheme. He called it good business. The first investors got their money when subsequent depositors added to the pot. Each time he took out huge profits for himself. Shame the investments never materialized as he had hoped. Wasn't that what investing in high risk/high return was all about? Everybody liked to gamble, but no one enjoyed losing. The penny-stock craze of the past decade fulfilled the same needs. No matter how dreary the financial outlook appeared there were always new clients frothing at the bit to sign over their money. Wasn't it W.C. Fields that said, "Never give a sucker an even break"?

Problem was the SEC didn't seem to agree. They claimed investors were 'duped' into giving Julian and Anders their money, when in truth they practically begged to have their money taken. Although Madoff ran off with the most money and the headlines, that didn't mean there weren't smaller fish in the Ponzi Sea. They'd just got caught swimming too close to the nets.

He arrived back home early in the afternoon. Ev's locked studio door didn't yield to his repeated knocking. A couple of afternoon drinks in his study later, he returned and shouted her name until she opened the door in a powder blue robe and a haggard look on her face.

"What?" she asked without malice. The lines in her unmade-up face seemed to be causing her pain.

"You complain that I'm never home. Well, I'm home and you lock yourself away."

"I'm supposed to turn my life on and off based on your schedule?" She spoke sluggishly, as if she were on some kind of medication.

He turned away and closed his eyes for five seconds before meeting her bored stare. "What would you say if I told you I'm supposed to die in eight days?"

She held his glance for a moment before an amused smile crossed her lips. She almost looked entertained. "That's a stretch, even for you."

"I'm serious." He wondered when the sparkle in her blue eyes had been replaced with the dull sheen of a polluted sky. "I went to this fortune teller and that's what he predicted."

"And you believe some quack in a turban and cape?" She turned to look away from him into the studio. Her head swiveled back and any joy she had found in his announcement faded like her youth.

"He predicted Digby's heart attack to the day."

"I could have predicted that, the way the man smoked and drank and ate." She pulled her robe tighter around her body.

"He knows things that he shouldn't."

"Haven't you always told me that you can make anything happen? Hell, you've bilked people in the financial markets for years and still come out looking squeaky clean. I'm supposed to believe you're going to let a carnival reject break your stride?"

"What if he's right?"

"Then you better hope your life insurance is paid up." She tapped her foot on the wooden studio floor. "Can I go back to work now?"

The emptiness in his gut nearly sucked the air from his lungs. "This guy has always been right. Doesn't it even bother you?"

"Ask me in eight days and I'll have a more formed opinion." She turned her back on him and closed the door. The last thing he heard was the metal lock sliding into place.

An hour later the news broke about Anders being a wanted man that had fled to Mexico. He thought about finding Ev and telling her about it. For some reason, she had a soft spot for the guy, claiming to admire his unwavering dedication. Perhaps in the la-di-da world of art circles her feelings were considered endearing. In the shark-infested business world it was a sign of weakness. If he died in eight days, she'd never make it without him.

*　　*　　*

Upon his return from Mexico, a tanned Anders was arrested amidst media fanfare. He forsook bail, even though he had the money to post it. By refusing council and opting to stay incarcerated, it appeared the man had given up hope. News agencies deemed his resignation as proof of guilt.

Julian wondered if the man's Christian values made their collective sins too much to bear. Anders once confessed that it didn't matter if their business practices fell under the scrutiny of the courts; they didn't warrant God's forgiveness. He resisted the urge to visit his old *compadre*. Best to let

13

the man take the heat and wait until things cooled down. And what about Renaldo's prediction? Could Anders feel betrayed and mad enough to try to kill him? That would be hard to do stuck in jail. Best to at least wait another week or so before visiting and not tempt fate.

His ex-partner had no next of kin, nor even any close friends he knew about. The investors only knew him as a voice at the other end of a phone line or via the Internet. So, if not Anders or the enraged 'stockholders', who else would want to kill him?

* * *

Julian spent the next seven days at home hiding from the rest of the world. If a bus was going to hit him or an airplane fall out of the sky, he wanted to make the target a little tougher. He refused to watch television and ignored his *Wall Street Journal*. The more disconnected the better. Both the cell phone and the computer stayed shut and powered down.

The lack of stimulation made the days interminable. Ev shut herself up in the studio, often sleeping on a cot next to her paints. If Renaldo's prediction came to fruition, he wondered how sorry she'd be for ignoring him during his last days. Her lack of concern for the predicament maddened him. Repeated banging on her studio door was met with silence. He once caught a glimpse of her in the kitchen just before she slipped back to the sanctuary of the studio. Late at night after too many drinks and not enough sleep, he pressed his ear to her door and swore he heard crying. He became a bitter, drunken stranger alone in his own house.

The more he thought about the prophecy of his impending death, the more he berated himself for succumbing to such weakness. A brooding gloom infested his mind. He didn't dare return to Renaldo's trailer. The note the man had left for him consumed many waking hours and bottles of brandy. How did the fortuneteller know he'd return? The dust that covered the crystal ball was as thick as that on the note. 'No one can protect you from yourself.' The ominous note inferred he was the instrument of his own death. A suicide? Only the powerless took that route.

He awoke on Saturday with a start. It was the thirteenth day since he spoke to the fortuneteller. The only thing he lay with in the sweaty sheets was the remnants of another fitful dream. A rational man would not let the ramblings of some curbside prophet affect his life. Still, Renaldo's track record in such matters left more then enough room for concern. What if the fortuneteller was right?

All he had to do was make it one more day. Twenty-four measly hours.

Ev hadn't shared their bed since their last argument a week ago. "To hell with her," he shouted to the walls. "She'll be sorry," the walls replied in his head as he did his best to face the day of his supposed demise with a positive attitude. Outside the sun glowed red with rage as it slowly climbed over the horizon. It was going to be the kind of day where minutes clawed to gang up and become hours. The hands of the clock seemed to constantly give him the finger.

Although the day refused to follow the conventions of time, nighttime finally assumed control. He found himself starting to relax, the past day aging him more than the passing of any seasons. Barring a heart attack, The Great Renaldo had turned out to be a fake.

At a quarter to midnight, he went to Ev's studio with two glasses of the finest single malt Scotch in hand. Of course, her door was locked, but he was so happy it didn't bother him. He just wanted to be with her, to share the stroke of midnight together. He'd admit the foolishness of Renaldo's prophecy and his own irrational fear. Promises to be a better husband filled his head. From now on, things would be different.

He pounded on the door, calling her name. "Ev! Ev! Open it. It's time to celebrate."

No answer. He pressed his ear to the door, but couldn't hear anything. He tried knocking again with no success. Feeling his agitation rise at her impertinence, he stormed off to get the skeleton key from his office.

He opened the door and burst into her studio. When he looked up, the sight made him sink to his knees and cry out to a God he knew looked down on him without pity. Evangelina hung from a wooden ceiling beam. The stain on the floor beneath her smelled of urine. A ladder had been used to tie the noose, and she'd apparently jumped and broken her neck before suffocation took her away. On the floor was his Wall Street Journal. Yesterday's headline screamed at him: Ponzi Schemer Commits Suicide. Anders' photo stared at him from the floor.

The smell of death had already begun to infiltrate the room. He screamed out her name. After his crying subsided, he looked up to see the still wet canvas on her easel. It was a picture completely different from what he had seen only a couple of weeks before. Reverting to a more classical mode, the painting showed two faces devoid of any surrealistic or abstract qualities. Everything was precise and perfectly constructed–the eyes that looked longingly at one another, the lips parted for a kiss, the arms and legs intertwined in a way that only passion could choreograph. It was the picture of a happy couple sitting under a full moon. The likeness was perfect: Evangelina and Anders.

When the last bit of the canvas had been burned, Julian called the police. As he sat in the studio hearing the sirens come closer, he could see the face of The Great Renaldo in his mind. He didn't laugh or cry. He just understood.

It was the day he died.

Nature's Way

Every two weeks, the Continental Livestock Auction sold off horses, cows, pigs and goats to the highest bidder. Howahkan Simchez, or Howard as he was known when not on the Reservation, climbed up the metal gate rungs to get a better view. Six horses jostled one another in the crowded pen. A light brown saddlebred with a majestic long neck had a gorgeous face, but obvious hoof problems. Three pintos of varying black and white color mixes were fighting over some of the hay in the paddock. Dozens of flies buzzed around each animal. With any luck he would find an affordable horse for his nine-year-old daughter.

There were about forty horses all told. Howard climbed up the fencing in the center of the pens to survey the other horses. A dark brown bay in the corner caught his eye. She looked to be older and about 15.2 hands. Not a huge horse, but solidly built. Navigating the metal bars separating the various pens, he dropped down into the section that held the Bay and three other horses. He waved off a mean palomino that left with a snort and pinned back ears.

The Bay looked at him and blinked its big brown eyes. Howard could see the horse was unsure, perhaps fearful. Why not? Humans were the horse's worst predator. As a Sioux Indian, he had a great respect for all animals. He grew up riding horses and appreciated their spiritual nature, dedication and beauty.

He patted the Bay's shoulder. The horse's ears moved back and forth. At least he had her attention. Good, she wasn't dead to the touch. Her temperament had passed the first test. He moved his hand slowly along her back. Air blew out her nose. His hand slid softly along her flank. He bent down and squeezed her right hock and the horse responded by lifting her leg for him. To his surprise, the foot was shod. At one time, someone had loved and cared for her.

After checking the horse's legs and confirmation, he continued the rudimentary exam on the Bay. Her muscles were taut and well developed but undernourished. The mane and tail were a little torn up but that was only cosmetic. Halfway through his evaluation the Bay licked and chewed to show her approval and even craned her head to playfully nuzzle him in thanks for the attention. In that moment he felt a bond, an understanding.

What was a good girl like her doing in a place like this? Although a lot of the horses in these pens were wonderful creatures, they were either very old, untrained, or had some kind of structural damage that deemed them useless in the eyes of those who once demanded their loyalty. For whatever reason that she was here, he felt it was a sign. She would be perfect for his Naida.

He casually scanned the pens to see if others were watching him, nervous that someone else might see in the Bay what he did. Above all of the pens was a rickety walkway where potential buyers could observe all of the livestock from a bird's eye view. The handful of cowboys and stragglers up there didn't seem to be looking his way. A group of four twenty-somethings—two boys and two girls—roamed the holding pens vocally assessing the horses within.

He climbed back to the front pen where three horses paced in tight circles. Across the dirt aisle was a pen with a single stallion bucking and snorting. A guy with a ruddy face and handlebar mustache stood gazing into the pen. Unruly chest hairs escaped from his fancy pink shirt. A huge belt buckle held up his workpants over which a voluminous stomach hung precariously. The man didn't look friendly. He seemed to size up the horse with calculating rather than caring eyes.

Howard hoped the guy didn't see him checking out the Bay. To throw him off, he began petting an old swayback quarter horse. The mare leaned its head gently on his shoulder. He continued to scratch as the horse closed its eyes and its lips began stretching away from its teeth in ecstasy.

"That's the last love that horse is ever going to see in this life." The voice came from a woman standing outside the pen. She was a wispy little thing, probably no more than five feet tall, a good foot shorter than Howard. She had straight white hair hanging down to her hips. Her figure was slight, almost devoid of curves in a loose-fitting T-shirt, but her blue eyes were clear and sharp. Weathered skin revealed she had spent a good amount of time outdoors. She had the aura of a hippie that never gave up the mantra of the Sixties but learned to live with reality.

Howard stroked the horse again, almost defensively. "She's a pretty old girl."

The woman smiled knowingly. "I know that horse. She's twenty-six years old. Spent most of her life schooling kids on a dude ranch in Wyoming. As each youngster learned, the next one got on her. She was a loving teacher and friend. When the last of the kids grew tired of her, the owners figured they couldn't sell her at that age so they sent her here.

18

Figured they could get a hundred or so bucks for her." She looked around the auction pens with obvious distaste. "This is the thanks she gets."

"It's a crime," he said to be polite. The last thing he needed was competition when the Bay in the back corner came up for bidding. A man of very limited means, the only way to get his daughter the horse she so richly deserved was through this auction.

"It's more than a crime. It's cruel and unnecessary. Those people could have put her out to pasture. They got the land and the money." She shook her head in disgust. "Nope. They figured they could squeeze the last dime out of her by sending her here."

He kept petting the swayback. "Will someone buy her?"

She shook her head once. "These horses are sold by the pound. Owners who feel these animals no longer serve a purpose discard them. They don't put any value on temperament, years of service, or ability to work. Most of the animals in these pens are going to be shipped off to either Canada or Mexico and turned into food for human consumption. Only a few will be funneled to another auction in hopes someone will buy them as a pasture pet or perhaps a work horse for three times what they fetch here."

The swayback got spooked when another horse kicked at her. She ran around the tiny pen with little room for escape. Howard climbed back over the bars to where the woman stood.

"Saw you eyeing that little beauty back there." She pointed towards the Bay.

"Naw," he said, trying not to sound alarmed. "Haven't seen anything good yet."

The woman smiled. "You don't have to worry about me. I'm not here to buy." She jerked a thumb over her shoulder without looking. "It's him you need to worry about."

Howard looked past her. On the bridge surveying the pens was a thin man with a pockmarked face in ill-fitting brown pants and a blue denim shirt with silver points at the collar tips. Even his ten-gallon cowboy hat couldn't shade his ugliness. "Who's that?"

"That's Ewan. Charlie Matchitehew's boy."

"Matchitehew. That's an Indian name."

"Could be," she said. "If so, then Charlie's tribe should scalp him for what he does for a living. He's one of the reasons I'm here."

He looked at her in a new light. His eyes begged a question that she picked up on.

"I work for a non-profit organization. It's called Angels Arrows. I keep track of the horses and how much they sell for. If I see any that are too weak or lame to survive the grueling trip to Mexico, my organization tries to

19

purchase them from the kill buyers to give them a humane death. There's no reason for these animals to suffer."

"Kill buyers?" Whatever they were, he didn't like the sound of it.

"That's what Charlie does. He and Dale Brewster are the guys who buy up most of these horses. If one of those guys gets an animal, it's going to be sold for meat."

He shook his head at the state of this great country that horses had helped to forge. How had Man come to cast aside the one creature that helped pave the way hundreds of years ago? They had always been a symbol of freedom and the power that came with it. Their strong legs and back kept humans solidly grounded in their spiritual path as they carried men and their burdens with dignity. And now we sell their flesh by the pound like garbage.

"If you want that horse," she said, disrupting his thoughts, "you'll need to register and get a bidding number."

"I'd like to get her for my daughter. She's nine."

"I'll take you over to the office to get you signed up."

He followed her as if she had a lead rope on him. By the time they reached the office, he learned her name was Sherri and that she was possibly his new hero.

*   *   *

The auction pit was in a barn-like circular building of wooden slats and smelled of livestock and sweat. In the center was a semicircle of dirt where the animals were paraded while being bid on. No one bothered to clean the occasional dung heap left behind. The bidders sat in wooden plank bleachers that slanted upwards surrounding the pit for maximum viewing. The auctioneer sat perched in a booth above the pit opposite the seating rattling amounts out so quickly Howard marveled at how the man could see the almost non-existent movement of hands and facial ticks used to place bids.

The auction worked its way through the pigs, often sold in groups of two and three. The animals were driven into the ring through a big sliding wooden door to the right of the auction booth. Above that door a digital sign gave the weight of the animal to be bid upon. A rustler moved the reluctant pigs using a tool with a plastic case on the end filled with rocks to sound like an angry rattlesnake. On the other side of the booth was a second large door where the animals were forced to go after bidding had finished. The screen over that door revealed the details of the winning bid. Each animal had a number on an oval yellow paper glued to his or her hindquarters.

After the pigs came the cows. Calves had been pulled from their mothers before being properly weaned. Some of them were dragged out of the ring by their ears. Howard understood the necessity of this business but found it difficult to contain his revulsion.

The first horse finally entered the ring just after the woman Sherri took a seat next to him. As a veteran of these sales she had agreed to bid for him and help get the horse for his daughter. She took out a pad to record the auction results. The auctioneer spoke so fast that the first horse sold before he could even figure out the bid amount.

Four horses were bought and sold when a bright-eyed mare was bullied into the ring. She was brown with two white front socks and a healthy, flowing mane. There were a couple of fresh cuts on her neck. The number pasted on her back read 6708. With fear in her eyes she limped into the center of the ring. Bidding lasted about fifteen seconds as the horse's life and fate were sold at sixteen cents per pound. At only 875 pounds, she sold for $140.

Howard looked around and saw the grotesquely fat man he'd seen earlier that day looking at the lone stallion. The guy leaned in one corner of the semicircle of seating near the entrance. The walrus mustache under his flat nose had more hair than his graying scalp. His thick arms were folded as he viewed the scene with an egotistical leer. Next to him was the thin guy Sherri had warned him about. Behind them were two guys in cowboy garb.

"See that guy in the pink shirt," Sherri whispered. "That's Charlie Matchitehew. His son is Ewan, the guy I showed you earlier. He does most of the actual bidding." She pointed to the opposite side of the room at a weathered man whose face looked as if smiling had been outlawed. "Over there is Dale Brewster. They're the kill buyers."

Howard stared at Charlie who leaned his girth against the concrete wall and handrail with careless abandon. He watched as the fat man purchased three more horses by barely lifting a finger.

"He doesn't look Native American," Howard whispered to Sherri while a 960 pound black horse with stifle problems sold for twenty-two cents a pound.

"He's no more Indian these days than I am," she said.

Howard had always been spiritually enlightened, but didn't believe in leaving things up to fate. Perhaps the man's Indian heritage would enable him to appreciate his pure intentions when bidding started on the Bay. What was one horse to this man? These beautiful animals were marks in a ledger book to him. Before Sherri could protest, he got up and made his way around the arena to Charlie.

"Excuse me, Mr. Matchitehew. Can I speak with you for a moment?"

21

The man didn't even look at him. "Kind of busy, buddy."

"My name is Howard Simchez. I believe we share Native American lineage."

Charlie continued to stare straight ahead.

Howard ignored the man's rudeness. "I'd like to ask you a favor. There's a mare coming up, #6727. I would like to buy her. My daughter needs a horse to learn how to ride and this is the only way I'll be able to afford it. I was hoping you would not bid against me to allow this horse to find a good home."

Charlie smirked. He finally turned to look at the man. "You're of American Indian descent?"

"Yes. Sioux."

"Mighty fine people." Charlie turned back to stare at the ring where a new horse was being brought in. He raised his hand and purchased the mare for sixteen cents a pound.

He hesitated to see if the man would say anything more. "Thanks," Howard said before returning to his seat.

"He's a bastard," Sherri said. "You can't trust him."

"Not a single horse has sold for more than twenty-two cents a pound. I should be able to get her for thirty cents at the most." He felt hopeful, excited for his daughter.

Ten minutes later the Bay was led into the ring. Howard looked over at Charlie, who hadn't moved since he had left. His cronies were talking behind him.

Bidding started almost immediately. The auctioneer asked for twenty cents. Howard turned to look at Sherri, who nodded him away. The opening bid price went down to fifteen cents per pound. Sherri raised her hand to bid. The auctioneer began sputtering words and numbers in machine gun staccato. Howard heard the number go to eighteen, and then twenty. Seconds past and the figure had gone into the thirties. As soon as Sherri put her hand up Charlie's son Ewan raised the bid. Before his brain could even comprehend what was happening the price escalated into the forties. He looked back desperately at Sherri. The bid was at fifty. She looked concerned and raised her hand a little tentatively to up the bid. He gazed over at Charlie, who still leaned with that self-satisfied grin on his face. When the bid went into the sixties, Sherri gave him a questioning look. The auctioneer asked for a higher bid. Howard wrestled with the figures in his brain and the painful result they gave him. The auctioneer gave a final warning. He helplessly shook his head back and forth. Sherri's shoulders sagged and she dipped her head as the auctioneer announced, "Sold for sixty-six cents per pound." More than three times that of any other horse. He looked over at Charlie. The obese man cocked his head with a smug smile

22

and spoke to the men behind him. He couldn't hear the words but he could read the big man's lips: "I'm such an ass-hole," the fat man said with obvious delight.

The terrified Bay took a step toward Howard. They locked eyes and he felt something inside curl up and die. A wrangler shook the rattlesnake tool at the Bay's hindquarters. She let forth a long yellow stream of urine that lasted about thirty seconds. The stable hand aggressively shooed the horse without letting her finish towards the far door to be shoved into a crowded pen to await the long transport to the slaughterhouse.

"Hey, Jerry, that should lower the sales price by a good ten pounds," Charlie shouted to the auctioneer.

"He just did it to be spiteful," she said. "He'll lose money he doesn't even have just to show he's the big man."

Howard couldn't speak. His stomach churned as he sat dumbfounded. For the remainder of the auction, he stared straight ahead with his lips pressed together. He refused to look at the rest of the horses as they passed one by one out the door from the chute, were paraded around the pit and ushered out. Sherri put a reassuring hand on his shoulder.

Leaving the auction and still dazed, he followed her outside into the dark parking lot. The horses were already being loaded into large double-decker trucks with ceilings so low only the ponies could put their heads in a normal, raised position. They crammed in as many as they could fit using cattle prods to move them onward. The sounds of their hooves on the metal floorboard amidst their whinnying made him sick.

"They'll drive over a thousand miles in there with no food or water," Sherri said. "A lot of them will get kicked or trampled. I've known of horses that died standing up on the trip."

Howard had to take a deep breath of the cool night air to keep from retching.

Charlie Matchitehew walked up to them with a smile surrounding the thick cigar in his mouth. "How you doing, kimosabee. Still interested in that brown mare?"

He stared at the big man with feelings of hatred and betrayal. "Why did you do that?"

Charlie took his cigar out and spit on the ground. "Do what?"

"I wanted that horse for my daughter. You only want her for meat. Why did you bid her away from me?"

"I tell you what, kimosabee. I'll sell her to you. Right here right now."

"You will?"

"Sure, man. Give me fifteen hundred for her and she's yours."

23

The sum was a sledgehammer crushing his chest. "That's more than twice what you bought her for."

"Yeah, well, a man's gotta make a living. Normally I'd ask two thousand. I'm giving her to you at a five hundred dollar discount, what you and me being almost kin and all."

"You are an evil man."

"And a bastard," Charlie said, obviously enjoying the situation. He didn't even acknowledge Sherri, who looked at him with repugnance.

"Come back in two weeks and we'll play some more." Charlie walked off laughing as his enormous gut jiggled up and down.

* * *

Charlie stopped at the Golden Corral for a steak after the horses were loaded and on their way. Hitting on the waitress that served him his Dr. Pepper proved futile. She gave him a look he long ago had stopped acknowledging. Before heading back to the Motel 6 he stopped by a liquor store. Picking up a six pack of Budweiser was a hell of a lot easier than the waitress. When he got into his room he laid back on the creaky bed and cracked open a brew. He didn't need the yellow pages to get some room service. He knew the number by heart.

The girl was somewhere in her low Twenties and plump. Her pudgy face had too much make up and she moved like one of the pigs down the chute at the auction. Fortunately, she wasn't much of a talker but luckily she was a groaner. It only took him a couple of minutes to finish.

"Can I have one of your beers?" she asked after he was done.

"Sure. That'll be two bucks."

She grimaced and got off the bed to collect her things and leave the room. He watched TV for about a half hour after her departure and polished off the six-pack before going to bed. Sleep came easily as he snored with a guttural rhythm. A little stream of drool rolled out of his jowl as he tossed and turned on the hard bed.

The door to his hotel room opened and a man walked in. He'd seen the man somewhere before but couldn't place him. Charlie lay paralyzed as the man tied both his wrists and ankles to the solid brass bedposts that he hadn't noticed when he checked in. The ropes were thick and dirty, the type he used to lead horses around with their halters. The room morphed into a corral with the bed at its center. The intruder stared down at him for a long while before opening up a pouch that was attached to his belt. From inside the small bag he removed some kind of talisman and placed it on the bed beside Charlie's head. He then pulled out two feathers and a vial of something red, perhaps blood. These also were laid on the bed.

24

The man pulled out a gleaming Bowie knife from a holster behind his back. With surgical precision, he sliced Charlie's right thumb clean off his hand. Without changing expression the man casually walked to the foot of the bed and sliced off both of his big toes. He stared right into Charlie's eyes as he came around the other side of the bed and chopped off the other thumb.

Charlie tried to break free but couldn't. However much he squirmed made the bonds grip tighter. The man leaned over and pulled the sheets away to expose his flaccid nakedness. Just as the knife was about to castrate him he screamed like the pigs he enjoyed slaughtering.

He woke bolt upright to the sound of pounding on the hotel walls and shouts from the room next door to shut the hell up. His bed was soaked. With sweat, not blood. He wiggled his ten toes and ten digits and waited for his pounding heart to relax.

*   *   *

Howard spent the days following the auction moping. His kids thought Mommy and Daddy must have been fighting because he went straight to bed after dinner each night. In the mornings he left the trailer before his wife awoke. At night when she tried to find out what was the matter he would shrug and say, "Nothing." She knew it was something about the auction that he wasn't ready to share.

Four days later he finished dinner and went into their bedroom. He came out a half hour later in his ceremonial clothes. His family stared at him in disbelief. These were sacred garments from another culture to his kids. When it came to their heritage, they were smart enough not to question the things they had yet to understand or appreciate. But, today was not a tribal holiday. His wife motioned for him to come outside so that they may speak in private. The time for silence had ended.

"You're going to see Billie," she said knowingly. Billie had been the tribe shaman ever since he was struck by lightning at the age of eleven. Many of the younger generation and even Howard's peers wrote the old man off as a loon.

Howard told her about what happened at the auction, how he had bonded with the magnificent Bay for Naida. He spoke of the light the horse kindled inside of him, and how Charlie the kill buyer had extinguished that flame out of spite. The desire to somehow hurt or get back at the fat man only made his shame greater. By now the horse was probably dead, but in his sleep he still saw its pleading brown eyes. Seeing Billie was the only way to allow both of their souls to rest.

"I only hope I will return as the same good man," he said with a bowed head.

His wife kissed him on each cheek with the certainty that he would.

* * *

Billie Eyota Angpetu, which meant "great radiant day" in the Sioux language, sat facing the healthy fire outside of his dilapidated trailer. His age was as timeless as the stars that shined above. Long black hair framed his wrinkled face, but in his eyes sparkled life as fresh as a new morning. He took a bite from the TV dinner that sat on a hot rock near the fire and chewed thoughtfully.

"You are a man of good soul, Howahkan" Billie said, using his tribal name meaning 'the mysterious voice.' "I know this not from what you tell me, but from what I feel in your presence and what I have seen in your lifetime."

Howard stared reverentially at the old man. Although there had never been actual proof of Billie's spiritual powers, a lot of strange and unexplainable occurrences had taken place in and around the area. There was the hunter who killed wolves for sport that was found torn to shreds inside his cabin. A tee-totaling moonshiner that peddled on the Reservation wound up drunk and died on the fender of a hit and run driver. Then there was the bank man who maliciously kicked families of Indians off of their land. He just disappeared one day.

"I see the Bay in my dreams," Howard said, his voice breaking with emotion. "She is running towards me. That horrible man, the kill buyer, is chasing her and laughing at us both."

"Is that all?"

Howard ducked his head. "In my dream I am in ceremonial paint, a warrior from the old times. My bow and arrow are poised and ready to shoot the man. When I let fly the arrow ends up striking the mare."

Billie nodded once. "Those who walk with the horse spirit seek awareness along paths they have yet to tread."

"I wanted the horse for my daughter. My going to that auction at that particular date and seeing that particular animal was…destined."

"And so it was. Just not as you foresaw it."

Howard watched the flames dance in the fire and felt the heat reaching out to him. "I cannot be whole until I have cleansed my soul of that horse's life force. Till I have done right by her and the bond we shared. I know it's stupid and childish, but–"

Billie held up his hand. "You felt her essence, and that is a gift. One not given or received lightly."

26

"All grand words, but they do nothing to soothe me. Bad things happen to good people, and men like that bastard…" He closed his eyes to quell the rising anger.

"You say his name is Charlie Matchitehew. That name means 'evil man.' A fitting title for one who callously plays God with a creature's life."

Howard shook his head in a futile gesture. He thought of Sherri and how despite her good intentions, hundreds of horses met horrible deaths at the kill buyers' hand every auction. And how many auctions were there in this vast country? "He mocks the life force. There must be something I can do to stop him from getting away with it."

"Perhaps your role in this human play is not as the champion, but the intermediary."

"For whom?"

Billie nodded at the fire. "Nature has a way of telling us when something is wrong. She also has a way of righting those wrongs, although we don't necessarily see or understand it. The tsunamis that wipe out thousands…did you ever think that those poor people living in squalor have gone to a more spiritually satisfying place?"

"But the Bay–"

"The Bay's path is its own, not yours."

Howard sat back and breathed in deeply. Maybe he was wrong in coming here after all. It had taken him nearly a week to gather up the courage, and now that he was here he felt silly. All they did was speak bloated declarations. Words to get drunk on and forget. Nothing could be done for the horse. What justice could be levied upon the kill buyer who hadn't acted illegally, just maliciously?

"Nature doesn't play favorites," Howard said looking down at his limp hands in the firelight. "I suppose my only choice is to live with reality as I cannot do anything to change it."

"You already have," Billie said. "Go home. Enjoy of your wife. Feel pride in your children. Your daughter and her horse will find each other. The natural state of all things is harmony. Find that inner peace and it will find you."

Howard left the trailer, and although his mind told him that nothing had been accomplished, his spirit felt at rest.

Billie methodically prepared his tools after Howahkan left. He failed to tell the younger man that the universe is a matrix of interdependence. He could not control the forces of nature, but he had the power to convince them to align themselves with the earth's soul. He worked all night with the wind at his back and the moon as his guide. Just as the sun awoke he retired to his trailer to let Nature take its cue.

The next Continental Livestock Auction took place on an overcast Wednesday. Eighty-three horses were packed into the dung-filled pens with enough food for about a quarter of them. There was no water, but the sky looked like it might oblige at any moment. Ewan Matchitehew had expected his father Charlie to show up an hour or so before the actual auction. They had already finished the goats and pigs and were onto the cows. He knew he could cover for his absent dad but had never done so at such a big auction and without explicit instructions. He gripped his buyer number in sweaty hands and lost a staring match with the clock on the wall over the auctioneer booth.

The first horse trotted into the ring. Standing in the very place his dad always occupied, Ewan gulped and put up his hand to bid. Dale Brewster at the other end of the room huffed with delight. Ewan had just bought the animal for the starting price of twenty cents a pound. He shouldn't have jumped the gun. He should have waited until the bid went down to fourteen cents.

The next horse came up. A thousand pound brown quarter horse. Dale bought the animal for only sixteen cents a pound; obviously amused that Ewan hadn't bid it up, as his father would have. As each horse came into the ring, he felt as if he made the wrong decision, either buying too high or getting out of the bidding too early. The sweat pasted his denim shirt to his back.

By the twentieth horse, he finally got into the swing of things. He got one up on Dale and let the man have a horse he knew was sickly. His confidence quickly grew into arrogance. His father's son. By the time they were half way through he was bidding like an old pro.

The next horse to enter the ring was a gelding so white it almost looked pink. It was the fattest horse of the day by far, weighing in at 1348 pounds. Something was wrong with its hooves. It didn't move well so the wrangler had to prod it into the ring. The creature's eyes looked terrified, as if it knew the fate that awaited it. The auctioneer hesitated a moment before getting the bidding started at fifteen cents a pound. He verbally tripped for the first time in years as the two kill buyers engaged in a bidding contest.

Charlie awoke to gazing faces staring down at him. His terrified eyes scanned the semi-circle of horseflesh buyers. He saw his son Ewan standing in the place he had bought countless horses from. Looking down he saw a pair of hooves, not feet. The dirt from the ring wafted up into his big nostrils. Someone yelled something in his direction. He turned his head in time to see the pit wrangler give him a massive kick. Each step he took around the auction pit hurt. Every time he tried to stop and stand still, he got a jolting smack.

Two men at opposite ends of the room were slowly raising the price higher—Dale Brewster and his son. In the middle of the arena he saw a familiar face. It was the guy from his dream, the one where he almost got his balls cut off. Maybe this still was the dream. Charlie tried to appeal to the man, to get him to outbid his son and the other kill buyer, but he just stared vacantly back at him. Then he recognized the face of the Sioux Indian who only two weeks ago had begged him to allow a horse to be purchased cheaply for his daughter.

Please raise your hand. Please bid for me. Don't let them kill me... Charlie wanted to say the words, but he couldn't. The numbers stalled at nineteen cents a pound. For a moment, he thought the Indian would save him and purchase him for his daughter, but he just got up and walked out of the arena as the auctioneer shouted, "Sold." Bidder #310 had won. That was his number, the one his son Ewan now raised high.

Charlie was herded into a putrid smelling truck with a slew of other frightened horses. A cattle prod jammed his back causing a spasm of pain. Once in the truck he couldn't move and could barely breathe. There was no food to calm him or water to cool him. A horse to his left kicked his leg while another hit him in the chest with such force he nearly dropped. Other horses bit him relentlessly. They were ganging up on him and soon stomping him to the ground. As the truck pulled away for its sixteen hundred mile drive, Charlie's soul cried out for mercy.

* * * * * * *

This story is dedicated to Horse #6727. Every year tens of thousands of horses are inhumanely butchered in Canada and Mexico for shipment overseas as a delicacy on some European or Japanese plate. These are magical creatures whose only crime is in trusting us humans and allowing themselves to be used for recreation, competition, and work. They are rewarded by being sold by the pound and shipped off amidst horrifying conditions to be killed in a painful and callous fashion thousands of miles from their homes. Please send a donation to one of the many groups that strive for the humane treatment of horses.

One Last Memory

Severin kicked the door open and pumped three rounds between the surprised eyes of the occupant on the toilet seat. The spasming body sprayed blood as he pushed it to the side of the stall. Cursing and spitting, he backed off and moved over to check the second stall. When he was sure of being alone, he shoved the gun back into his pants and pissed on his fresh kill, watching with grim detachment at the dispersing flies. The sticky liquid of another life seeped onto his toes through the hole in his old combat boots.

Not a single shard of mirror remained in the frame above the sink. The dull metal reflected the blurred image of a man, his face a distant memory in a sea of images, most of which were best forgotten. The faucet creaked as he turned it. Cold water spat out. He used one hand to hold down the spigot while splashing his face with the other. It had gotten to the point where nothing could make him clean. Sometimes he wondered if his fallen comrades were the lucky ones.

For years he roamed the outskirts of what was left of the towns, foraging the ruins for sustenance and shelter. Occasionally, he'd come across someone like himself hiding in the burnt out buildings or camouflaged in a makeshift camp inside one of the craters left behind care of the fighter planes. But they were always worse off than he, and the last thing a man trying to stay afloat needed was to grab onto another drowning man. His only goal was to stay alive.

With a wheezing exhale of breath, he pushed open the bathroom door. The desolation of the outside world no longer sent a shiver down his aching spine. Because of the fallout the sun hadn't made a cameo appearance in months. Dust devils chased leaves across the cracked pavement. He shielded his face from the wind that rattled the three bodies that hung like frozen chimes slung from the scarred and barren tree. Walking closer to get a better look at the naked men, he noticed even the flies strayed from the putrid carcasses, opting to take turns dive-bombing the fecal matter below. The shocking part was not the state of the men, but their presence here.

The first shot ripped his heavy coat and tore skin off his shoulder. *Should've heard them coming*, he thought as he scrambled around the corner of a wooden tool shed. The shot had come from above, as usual. He grimaced as he gazed down at the blood seeping onto his dirty jacket. *Have to get that cauterized.* Had he actually said that or just thought it? It had been so long since he'd connected with someone. Had he become one of those addled war casualties like in the Rambo movies he and his wife used to make fun of? His face softened at the thought of...oh, god. What was her name again? Addie, that was it. He began to close his eyes when a second shot splintered the wood just above his head.

He rolled to his left away from the bullet's trajectory. Warning sounds boomed through the air. Somewhere on the horizon were their crafts. The darkening skies helped conceal his pursuers, but he knew from hunting as a boy that prey rarely saw its executioner.

Four old fuel pumps jutted out of the ground, the tombstones of a dead culture. The old filling station had probably seen better days, but then so had he. Although he could no longer see the hanging corpses, those people must have lived here. How long had they been holed up before being tracked down?

Aside from the shed, the house and attached filling station were the only above ground buildings for miles. He knew his only chance for survival depended on getting inside. The distance between the shed and the main structure looked to be about fifty yards. His mind clicked back to being a football player as a kid, and how they used to run these distances all afternoon in full pads. With a few quick breaths, he prepared for a burst of speed. Before making his move, his head darted in each direction and above, searching for snipers. Dispensing with a now useless prayer, he burst out into the open, running slightly serpentine to dodge potential bullets. His chest burned from the effort. Although no shots had been fired, he dove the last few yards and rolled to the edge of the house.

The wound in his shoulder began to throb as he leaned along the wall. He followed it to a door leading into the garage, expecting a gunshot to burn his tired body at any moment. Heaving his good shoulder into the unrelenting wood rattled him. *Damn it!* There had to be another way in. Any moment another volley of gunfire could take him out. Slumping down against the wall, he buried his head in his hands and succumbed to a cerebral suicide–he thought about the past.

A memory blipped in his brain. Once, he had a wife and two children. A home. And work that didn't involve firearms. His hands began to tap lightly on his thighs, the fingers moving in separate yet fluid motions. Even without keys to respond to his touch, he could hear the mellifluous notes and feel the music carry him away as it had so many times in his dreams. He recalled being able to make his piano bring a concert hall to rapture or tears. Now, the only notes his fingers could tap out were the

31

monotone sounds of a gun blast. It wasn't that he minded the killing. That had become as essential as breathing. What bothered him was the lack of any future. He had fought for his family in hopes that one day they could live in a world where pianos made music again and people formed a community. If the war ever ended, he couldn't go home—the word didn't mean anything anymore.

It seemed he'd been on the run for more than one life. Less than forever, but pretty damn close. And the fatigue. How long had it been since he'd been able to steal a few hours of pure sleep? To be able to drift off and dream instead of dozing with one eye open and an itchy finger on the trigger. What did it feel like to touch another human being instead of a cold hunk of metal? He began to fall asleep until a barrage of shots ricocheted off the ground between his legs.

A computer-generated pronouncement of warning from above hit him like an ordnance burst. He crawled furiously along the garage's perimeter towards the connected living area. The cold of the ground competed with the thick air to make him even more miserable. But, shivering was feeling, and even a bad feeling made him smile. It meant he was still alive.

He smelled cooked food from inside the house. If the people strung up outside were the former inhabitants, then who was living there now? The aroma of fried meat in thick grease teased his nose. Fresh bread whispered a love song to his empty stomach. When was the last time he ate prepared food?

Approaching aircrafts hummed over the lonely whine of the breeze threading through the junkyard behind the house. He needed to get inside. His breath escaped from his mouth in desperate smoke signals. "Every breath we let go into the air," the Sergeant once told him, "is a piece of our soul escaping the bonds of earth. When nothing comes out anymore, then we're finally free." Severin wondered how many more deposits to the Infinite he had left.

He shimmied along the outside of the building and around another corner. No shots accompanied his new perspective, so he stood up and assessed the structure. A four-foot wide aluminum foil tube fed into the house like an umbilical cord from a large generator. Whatever was inside couldn't be worse than what he faced out here. A quick slice with his buck knife in the cylindrical wall of the tube gained him access. He slid inside, holding his nose against the chemical odor.

The tube led into a type of computer room, though the room had probably once been a barn. The equipment was low-tech, though it still looked odd given the decrepit exterior of the gas station and home. A low electrical hum masked the noise of the outside world. The mainframe panels were foreign to him, engraved in a language he couldn't fathom. An enormous fan in the corner cooled the processors. He pushed open the heavy metal door at the far end of the room and found himself in a long, uncarpeted hallway with closed doors on both sides. The living quarters.

The dwelling still had that pre-war feel. The hallway paint was a dull yellow. Dirt masked the natural grain of the wooden floor. Clean square areas about eye level revealed that pictures used to hang there. Were they family pictures hastily grabbed at the time of the invasion?

Joyful shouts startled him into a defensive crouching position. They came from somewhere down the hall. Were they ghosts of a memory or did he really hear them? The revelry filled the hall again. Youngsters were having fun. Surely they must have heard the approaching war ships and the shooting. Why weren't they hiding?

More blissful shrieks. They sounded about as old as his kids were before the war. How old would they be now had they survived? Would they have become soldiers? He whipped his head back and forth to banish the thoughts. He had to survive as if they still mattered. Somewhere, someone else's children might benefit from his struggles. That was what usually kept him going.

With practiced care, he crept down the hallway. In one swift motion the knife with the long soiled blade slid deftly into his left hand, keeping his right hand free to draw his gun. As he advanced toward the sound of the young ones, a whimper to his right distracted him. He froze until he heard the helpless whine again. Outside of the house he heard the artillery maneuvering and the smaller attack ships disembarking from the mother ship. The foot soldiers wouldn't be far behind.

The exquisite smell of cooking food tormented his empty stomach. He swallowed hard and concentrated on the whimpering sound behind the door at the end of the hall. He placed his hand on the knob and turned it slowly. The door opened with a small squeak. Inside the small, warm room a baby lay on its back squirming to stand up. Arms and legs splayed while its head lulled about. It may have looked innocent, but he knew it would one day learn what all of these youngsters learned: how to track down and kill.

A click came from behind him. He reeled around with the gun already drawn to get a bead on the origin of the sound. It was only a synchronized wall unit. It flashed a blue and purple light, whizzed and clicked again. The infant gurgled. He approached it and looked into its questioning eyes. A wave of pain passed through his body. The wound in his shoulder needed attention. The baby made another noise and reached out for him. He leaned over the child brandishing the knife. With a grimace, he thrust the blade through its throat. Just then, the door behind him opened.

Spray from the knife's wound mingled with the sweat on his face. Severin pulled the knife out and whirled around. The baby's blood dripped off the blade onto the floor. Through his haze of tears, he saw three young ones. Their eyes begged a question.

"It'll never learn to hate me." His voice sounded foreign to his ears. Rusty vocal chords made the sentence come out hoarse. The three siblings stood blinking at him, unable to communicate with the intruder with the bloody knife hovering over their kin. He wanted to say something more, but couldn't. *What good is talking in a world that can't listen?*

From outside the house a computer generated voice demanded surrender. They had the building surrounded. He'd wasted too much time. The sound of mechanical clamor outside told him the ground forces had been deployed. Trapped. No way to escape now. The siblings stood there mesmerized. A piercing wail cut through the air. His gun hand came up reflexively, the index finger nestled comfortably on the trigger. Without emotion he pulled the trigger once, twice, a third time. The report of each shot was accompanied by the sound of ripping flesh.

Rather than stick around to listen to their death songs, Severin stepped over the mound of the three writhing siblings. The floor was slippery with their blood. Back in the hallway, he could hear the parents lumbering towards him though he couldn't see them. His nose led him towards the cooking smell. Meat. Sustenance. If this old house were to be his grave, he'd at least like a last meal.

A shadow loomed around the corner. The eldest of the clan? Severin flattened his body against the wall and waited. The shadow materialized—the mother. He needed only a second to leap at her and introduce his blade to her jugular. She was a big one. As she crumpled to the ground he recognized the resemblance to the kids he'd just slain in the other room. The father wouldn't be far behind. A whiff of the sizzling meat beckoned him with an unspoken promise. He cast the mother's body aside and barged carelessly through the door into the kitchen.

Once inside the cooking area, he barricaded the entrance. Heavy movement on the other side of the door signaled the father's approach. Perspiration prickled his body from the heat of the ovens and gas stove. The grey dusk crept into the room through a single, circular window. A spray of ordnance splintered through the walls and sent him diving for the floor. Pain blazed in his leg and side.

A blast somewhere in the house knocked him over just as he tried standing up. The hearing in both ears cut out. *One moment of solitude—that's all a man could hope for.* With that thought as his crutch, he painfully rose to a standing position. His line of sight came level with the sizzling meat. He licked his wind-cracked lips. Oblivious to the searing pain, he dipped his

34

hand into the boiling grease and pulled out a hunk. Blowing furiously to cool it down, the meat dangled between his fingers. Mouth-watering grease spattered onto the floor.

On the other side of the bolted door, the father pounded and made screeching sounds at him. Another mortar round riddled the building. The wall wouldn't hold much longer. He tasted the succulent morsel in his hands and closed his eyes. He didn't want to waste one iota of the pleasure the real food gave him. The meat tasted tender and juicy, and he savored the way his stomach welcomed it. He shoveled in another piece and then another. The meat caressed his tongue with flavors he'd long forgotten.

"The world is a time bomb and we are the fuses," he remembered the Sergeant telling him. When he opened his eyes he knew his lit fuse neared the charge. A recognizable object floated to the surface of the broth in the huge soup vat at the back of the stove. His stomach lurched violently. The bubbling liquid spun the bulbous orb around. Just as the kitchen door burst open behind him and the walls became rubble, he stared directly into the inert eyes of a face bobbing in the soup.

Severin didn't have time to vomit. They were upon him from all sides. Razor-like steel from the father's thirteen incisors pierced through his body. Suction cup tentacles drained whatever blood hadn't already spurted out. Pain—the final emotion—filled his brain as the invading aliens finally triumphed over the last remaining human on earth.

The Wedding Present

Cole Deekins fixed his stare at the Triple G Saloon and spit into the muddy, dung-filled street of Hawkins deep in the Dakota Territory. The afternoon sun beat down, daring any man to challenge its authority. Two miners carried out a drunken third between them as Cole pushed open the saloon doors. Inside the two-story wooden structure, the card games were about as clean as the whores and the whiskey, but he never had been a very clean man. A barely audible piano accompanied the racket of human livestock. Realizing he was skint for funds, he turned away unsated from the Triple G and headed back to his dry goods store around the corner of Main Street.

Deekins & Higson Dry Goods was also two-storied, but filled with the tools a man could lay his hands on without having to let go after paying for them. For five bits an axe or a saw could be purchased. Metal pans cost two. Two weeks ago, the plot of land was a mud puddle. But then again, two months ago Hawkins was wilderness. Gold had a funny way of populating places.

Cole and his partner Cyrus Higson had built the store out of wood and nails, using the upstairs as both storage and sleeping quarters. Cy was a Jew, and knew not only how to make a buck, but how to hang on to it. They'd met in Cheyenne in 1876. Some loud-mouthed young buck with more whiskey in his brain than common sense tried to cheat him on a purchase of a saddle. Cy tried to step in and smooth things over. The young buck pulled a gun and Cole was forced to waste two good bullets on the bastard. They'd been partnered going on three years now.

Cy hailed from New York. The prospect of a new world on the frontier lured him out west. Though slim of build and unskilled in the ways of the gun, his amiable conversation and keen sense of propriety endeared him to Cole. This was a man who could make something solid of his life, someone to anchor a dream onto.

In the early 1870s Cole rode with a loose band on the prairies butchering Indians for ten dollars per-head. In '75 he accompanied Captain Leander McNelly when they crossed the Mexican border illegally in pursuit of General Juan Cortina and his cattle rustlers. He'd killed a few men's share of Indians and Mexicans. His speed with a gun was only matched by his temper. Two failed marriages, one in his hometown of Richmond, VA, and one in Cheyenne, showed his inability to settle down. It was his pending divorce in Cheyenne that hastened his departure for Hawkins, a town with fewer laws than outlaws.

When he reached his dry goods store, he found the front door bolted. He tried to spit on the ground, but his mouth was too dry. The shop was supposed to be open. Although most purchases were made early in the morning as the miners made their way to their claims or late in the evening after a day of prospecting, afternoon trade occasionally brought in some cash. Using his key, he unlatched the door and pushed it open.

The smell of the pine used to build the place still hung in the air. Behind the counter at the far end of the store, near where they kept the till, the sound of a board creaked back and forth. *Squeak-a, squeak-a, squeak*-a. Cole drew his gun. No rat could make that big a sound. And the other kind of varmint foolish enough to draw on him would end up a stain on the floor. Crouching, he angled in towards the counter, gun pointing the way.

"Come on out of there," he called.

The creaking wood stopped, following by heavy breathing. The smell of someone else's sweat filled his nose.

"Don't try nothin' lessen you want to end up dead." His finger stroked the trigger.

"Cole?" came a voice from behind the counter. Half of Cy's naked torso peeked out, his bird's nest of brown hair even more disheveled than usual. His clean-shaven face, which made him look even younger than his twenty-six years, smiled stupidly at his partner. "Don't shoot me, hoss." He playfully raised his hands in mock surrender. "I'm unarmed." The sound of a female giggle made his smile even wider, his crooked teeth a tatty wooden bridge over the ravine of his mouth. "In fact, I'm undressed."

"Goddamnit, Cy."

The counter hid Cy from the waist down. Blond hair, stringy and wet, bobbed up and down the horizon of the counter. Cy's eyes went dull as he opened his mouth with a small groan of pleasure.

Cole stared at his partner and grimaced before turning around to leave the store. He heard a sound akin to pigs eating their slop and felt a pang in his loins. Before opening the front door, he called over his shoulder. "I'll come back after lunch." He closed the door and headed into the parched afternoon.

*   *   *

Thirty minutes later, after a drink on credit and a throw with Merrill, the big, buxom brunette that always let him stay a few minutes after he blew his load, Cole moseyed back to his store. He walked into the open door and saw Cy leaning back in a chair, his boots high on the counter.

"Afternoon, amigo," Cy said.

"Afternoon."

"Sorry about earlier."

Cole took off his wide brim black hat and lay it down on the counter next to Cy's feet. Reaching into his waistcoat pocket, he located a bit of snuff and stuck in into his mouth.

"You remember Darlene?" Cy asked.

Darlene. The girl from the Triple G. She'd come in on the coach about six weeks ago with the new shipment of whores from Chicago. Kind of pretty, with little titties but a big ol' smile and long, slender fingers. He hadn't had her yet.

"Sure," Cole said.

Cy slid his feet off the counter. "I asked her to marry me."

Cole spit some chaw into the spittoon by the counter. "Why?"

"Why?" Cy laughed and stood up. The wooden counter separated them. "Why not?"

"Hell of a reason for having to feed two mouths." All Cole had ever wanted was a warm woman and a cold bath. Usually one out of two sufficed.

Cy shrugged off his partner's gruffness. "Well, then, because I love her. And I think she loves me."

Cole's gaze remained fixed and serene. That had been one of his best traits, why he'd won so many gunfights. He didn't show much emotion. The women initially loved him for it, especially his two wives. Eventually, they hated him for the very same characteristic. As for love, more men had died because of it than lived. "She loves the trade."

"You cocksucker."

Cole heard fumbling under the counter. Without moving he watched as Cy clumsily hefted a Colt .38. He blinked once and spit out another stream of chew.

"I'll hold you to accounts for that remark," Cy said, his voice wavering as much as the gun.

"My land, Cy. Why you want and go and do that for?"

"I don't appreciate what you said about Darlene."

Cole leaned on the counter towards his partner, the gun only a hand's reach from his face. "I don't mean nothin' by it. I just don't know why you want to go and marry one of Barton's whores."

Barton owned the Triple G. He was a broad shouldered man with a long mane of black hair. He'd once caught a cowboy trying to shove the broken pommel from a saddle into one of his whores and beat the man's head to a bloody pulp with it. The blood still stained the floor of the room. Barton didn't treat his girls much better. Flora, Cole's favorite, constantly sported welts on her back, care of the whippings Barton parceled out to keep her in line. All anybody knew was that he killed a man back east, though Cole was pretty sure he'd killed quite a few out west as well.

"I'm going to make an honest woman of her," Cy said.

Cole raised a flat hand and motioned at Cy to lower the gun. "I didn't say nothing about her being honest or not. In fact, a whore's is probably the most honest profession in this territory."

Cy holstered his gun as awkwardly as he'd pulled it. "Cocksucker." This time he said it without malice.

"How much is it gonna cost us?"

Barton owned his women, as did any cathouse proprietor. The girls got a small percentage of the money they brought in. Since blowjobs cost two bucks and fucking cost five, Cole wondered what he'd charge for losing a lifetime of whore money.

"Said he'd cut her loose for four hundred."

The amount was staggering, but Cole didn't flinch. "We got four hundred?"

"Yeah." Cy leaned both hands on the counter. "I'll owe ya. But, I'm good for it."

He didn't care about the money. Hell, Cy'd made them much more than he could have made on his own. "Barton's a vindictive son of a bitch. You really think he'd sell one of his girls to a Jew?"

"Said he would." Cy had long ceased taking offense to slurs on his religion. If he had challenged men for insulting his heritage, he'd have been dead before he'd ever met his partner.

"I don't trust him." Cole once caught one of Barton's dealers cheating, and pulled a gun on him. Barton stepped in. They scrapped, with Cole getting the better of the saloon owner. Until one of Barton's men clubbed him and he woke up a mile out of the settlement, half naked and freezing his nuts off. Their relationship hadn't improved since then.

"Said he'd take four hundred."

Cole hunched his shoulders. He couldn't argue with Cy. Well, he could argue, but he could never win. "Both of my wives were whores. They just didn't get paid for it." He stood up and offered his hand. "Congratulations."

* * *

Cole sat hunched over the bar at the Triple G staring into the amber whiskey in his glass. Next to his arm sat the half-full bottle ready to accommodate his every whim. The best thing about saloons was the smell. Instead of the piss, shit, and dead animal stench of the town, the bar reeked of sawdust and sweat tempered by lilac perfume from the whores. It smelled like success to him. Stokes, the bartender, kept eyeing him. Probably on orders from Barton. In Hawkins, if you didn't have someone watching your back, more than likely you'd end up with a knife in it.

It was nearly as hot inside the saloon in the evening as it was in the daytime. Outside, the moon peeked suspiciously around the clouds, as if it didn't want to miss whatever was about to happen. The place was quiet for nine o'clock. Even the piano in the corner remained silent. The wood chips on the saloon's floor hadn't been swept. The clientele often paid in gold dust measured at the bar, so Barton kept the sawdust heavy to mask any fallen bits and residue, which got swept up and siphoned out. The claims hadn't yielded much gold this week, so trade was down. The girls offered throws at a dollar discount, but when you were low on funds, less was still more than most could afford.

As he cradled his glass, he tried to figure out what he could buy for Cy as a wedding present. Most everything worth anything came from their store. Cy wasn't much of a drinking man. Beside, a bottle of liquor didn't seem a proper gesture to a man marrying a whore. His partner had no use for a better gun than the .38 Colt he already had. No, he needed something special. Something to let him know how much he was appreciated, and how he hoped his partner would be happy.

The level of the bottle lowered steadily. Sometime during the evening, a piano player showed up and belted out rag after rag. A raucous group of cowboys took up two of the wooden tables, drinking and singing songs no one else wanted to hear. They kept the girls busy, though. In the corner of the room, a civilized card game played out between two men dressed like preachers and a couple of roustabouts.

Darlene meandered a few stools down from where he sat. She was a rugged girl with the kind of strong hips women needed to survive out west. Her modest bosom squeezed tightly into the dirty beige dress. Her face reminded him of the bedrolls they sold in the store—worn, but comfortable.

He sneezed, the ever-present haze of dirt and cheap tobacco smoke tickling his nose. The bar counter had a constant film of light brown, no matter how many times Stokes wiped it clean with his dirty rag. "Hey, Darlene." He motioned with his head for her to join him.

She looked around and weighed her options before closing the distance between them, leaning back on the bar and jutting her chest out. "Hey, Cole."

"Drink?"

Her eyes gave the bottle a once-over. "Sure." She smelled of gin and some kind of vinegary honeysuckle.

Cole motioned for Stokes to bring him another glass, which he filled to the brim before refilling his own. The bottle felt painfully light. He handed the shot to her and raised his glass. "To you and Cy."

Darlene eyed him suspiciously for a moment, and then downed her shot. "You want a throw?"

"Nope."

She scratched at her armpit and then tipped the shot glass to her mouth to make sure it was completely empty.

"You gonna miss the life?" he asked.

"I ain't dyin'," she said as she slammed the glass on the counter. "Just gettin' married."

Cole nodded.

"Thanks for the drink." She pushed off the bar and made a slow circuit around the room, deliberately sticking her ass in any face close enough to see it.

Next thing he knew, his bottle lay empty on the bar. The gaslights of the Triple G seemed to radiate heat out of their sconces. A fight broke out at the card table. He could hear the raised voices and the smashing of chairs. He staggered to his feet and made his way to the saloon doors. Just before he pushed them open, he stopped. Turning around, he ambled back up to the bar.

"Hey, Stokes."

The burly man with a face full of grizzly hair warily sauntered up to him, wiping out a glass with the same dirty rag he used on the bar. "Yeah."

"I want to talk to Barton."

"What about."

"Darlene."

"What about her?"

"How much he charge to get her for the entire night?"

*   *   *

Cy woke up early in the morning and walked out into the street of Hawkins. Even at this early hour, the smell of excrement, frying meat, dirty laundry and decay battled for supremacy. He hadn't slept well, full of both anxiety and anticipation. Last night was Darlene's final one working for that bastard Barton and the Triple G Saloon. No more would strange men be sticking their business in her, or grabbing her hair as her mouth gorged their

41

members. She'd be able to walk the streets in a couple of months without people catcalling.

The four hundred dollars burned a hole in his pocket. A hell of a lot of money. But, what was a person's life worth? In Hawkins, not much. One day you might be down to your last nickel. The next, you could either be the richest man in the territory or lying face down in the creek staining the rocks red. The territory buried as many men as dreams. Maybe more.

He wasn't about to let the west defeat him. Or mold him. The gun may have been the way of the town, but someday soon knowledge would be the voice that controlled the weapon. And he was smarter than all of the liars and thieves that populated this town. As he made his way to the Triple G, he wondered where his partner had slept last night. Usually, they bunked above the store, Cole snoring like a buffalo. He hadn't thought much about where he and Darlene would live, but first things first.

He pushed open the doors of the saloon. No one was at the bar. A couple of slumbering bodies littered the floor next to knocked-over chairs. A thick haze of dust hovered. Shafts of sunlight stabbed through the slats of the wooden door. The smell of whiskey and puke almost made him retch. None of the girls were around. Probably all sleeping off the night's work.

A bottle sat on the bar, the only thing still standing. Two fingers of whiskey remained. Eyebrows raised, he grabbed the bottle by the neck. How often did you find free liquor in a saloon? Cy figured the drink must be some kind of good omen for Darlene's first day as his woman.

He sauntered with the bottle over to a corner table, his boots making heavy scraping sounds on the wooden floorboards. Reckoning he'd have to wait a good hour for Barton, he righted a chair to sit where he could view the four rooms to the back of the saloon where the girls plied their trade. His restlessness got the best of him as he downed the whiskey in two gulps. Right after polishing off the bottle, he heard a squeak of hinges. A door opened at the far end of the hall. He tipped up his hat up to get a clearer view. A giggling Darlene walked out of the room. Before he could kick his feet down from the table and call for her, he saw Cole following her. They hurried out the back of the saloon.

Cy planted his feet on the ground as his hand firmly gripped his Colt .38.

*   *   *

Cole got back to the store just after eighty-thirty in the morning. Surprised that Cy wasn't there, he set about preparing the store for opening. He swept the floor, pulled up the shutters, and set out samples for the customers to inspect. Where the hell was Cy? If they hoped to cover the

42

four hundred they were dishing out for Darlene, they'd need to sell some stock.

Darlene wasn't the marrying type. What the hell did Cy think she was going to do all day? Darn socks and cook him meals? This was the Dakota Territory. The only job she knew was whoring. Her defection would no doubt disappoint a lot of the town. The whores saved more men than the Doc and the preacher combined.

He heated up some coffee, setting out two tins in case his partner showed up.

* * *

"She's had more men in her than an outhouse," Barton said, leaning back on his chair in the second floor office above the saloon. He had a pitted face that gave the moon a run for its money. Unshaven and still in his white long johns, he cracked open a bottle of whiskey and took a confident slug.

Cy seethed with anger. His taut lips covered gritted teeth.

"You look drunk," Barton said.

"What if I am?"

Barton set the bottle on his desk between them and leaned forward, the chair squeaking in protest. "I thought Jews didn't drink the whiskey. Thought you all were more into wine and such."

"We drink whiskey. When we need to."

"You got the money?"

"I do."

Barton's eyes never left Cy. His arm slowly extended forward, the uncurling hand a request for payment.

Cy reached into his pocket and pulled out the bills; four hundred dollars in tens, fives, twos, and ones. He tossed it off-handedly onto the desk. The sounds of the town awakening dented the silence of the room. Horses whinnied, men yelled, and the occasional wheel cart jostled by.

"In my hand." Barton's eyes remained riveted on Cy.

Gulping hard and nearly shaking with rage, Cy leaned forward and grabbed the wad of bills. He hesitated, licking his lips once, before placing the money into the open palm. He let out a breath and sat back in the wooden chair.

Barton's fist closed around the cash. "You just bought the best blow job west of the Mississippi. Just ask your partner." He didn't smile, nor did he offer Cy a drink.

"She's mine, then?" Cy asked, struggling to remain composed.

"You're her owner. Not sure if you'll be her keeper."

43

* * *

By nine-thirty, Cole had waited long enough. Maybe Cy was at the Triple G, starting his honeymoon before the wedding. Well, there was still work to be done. Pussy had to wait. With the new shipment of tools due to arrive today, he needed Cy to deal with the accounts.

Or maybe Cy ran into trouble with Barton. The bastard would prey on his partner's weakness. Before strapping on his Colt .45s, he made sure they were both ready for action. There were worse ways to start your day aside from shooting Barton. He locked up the store and went in search of his partner.

He saw Cy burst through the saloon doors. About forty yards separated them. His partner was not taken to violence, but he had a look of determination. Raising a hand in greeting, he called out. "Cy. How'd it go?"

Cy's head lowered like a bull preparing to charge. He moved forward with his hands at his sides. The fingers were cupped and twitching, like a man working up to a gunfight.

Cole stopped short. "Cy?"

"Draw, you son of a bitch."

Cole stretched out his hands wide in surrender. "What's goin' on?"

Twenty yards separated the two men.

"You lousy son of a bitch." Cy sloppily reached for the gun in the holster.

One of Cole's hands reflexively moved to his hip where the Colt .45 Peacemaker, a holdover from his days with McNelly, waited patiently. The other reached out in a 'stop' motion. "Talk to me, Cy."

"Talk to this." Cy's gun came up and exploded.

Cole didn't want to move, but his hand couldn't help it. Cy's bullet landed far from the mark. In a flash, the Peacemaker nestled in his hand and his finger pulled the trigger.

Cy froze. The fire drained from his eyes as blood spilled out of the hole in his chest and stained his white shirt. His gun arm lowered and he shot into the ground. Dropping to his knees, his face softened into a plea.

Cole took a step forward. Cy fell face first into the mud.

A crowd began to gather. Cole ran to his friend and went onto his knees. Rolling him over, he saw a red river gushing from his chest. He shook his friend. "Goddamnit, Cy. Goddamnit."

"Why?" Cy spluttered through the blood flowing out of his mouth.

"Why what?"

"Why Darlene? Why did you have to have Darlene?"

44

Cole wanted to hide his head deep below the dung of this godforsaken town. "I didn't have Darlene."

"I saw you…" Cy choked as he coughed up more blood. "It was her last night."

Cole shook his head. "It was supposed to be your present."

"Betrayed," Cy managed to get out, the breaths becoming more labored. "My friend…"

"I bought her…" Cole looked into his friend's fading and tear-stained eyes. "…So she wouldn't turn any more tricks on her last night. We played cards. Hell, she even beat me out of ten dollars."

Cy tried to laugh, but couldn't manage it. He made a few gurgling noises before his body shuddered and gave out. Dead eyes stared blindly as the blood continued to flow onto Cole's hands.

He lay his friend's body gently down in the street. When he looked up, he saw Darlene standing over them. She blinked a couple of times and shrugged her shoulders.

"That it?" he asked her

"That what?" She turned her back and lifted a hand to cover her eyes from the glare of the rising sun as she traipsed back to the Triple G.

One of the countless flies that infested the town landed on Cole's trigger finger. He dropped his gun into the mud and blood pooling at his knees. The buzzing fly left to join the horde taking interest in Cy's dead body before settling back on his gun hand. He didn't have the strength to kill it.

Love Scars

Benoit loved Celia Valieri the moment she walked into the hospital consultation. His powder blue issue scrubs provided a plausible alibi to be in the waiting room where the Valieris signed in to see the New York hospital's foremost obstetrician. Celia moved with such effortless grace across the room. A wave of silky brown hair framed a face that glowed with youthful exuberance. While she signed the register for her appointment, her husband picked up an old *Sports Illustrated* and sat heavily into a chair. He was a solid man with chiseled good looks and unshaven face like those Latin singers Benoit saw on CD covers at the Target.

He picked up the clipboard to memorize the neatly printed VALIERI on the sign-in sheet. The nurse behind the counter frowned and narrowed her eyes at him. He gave an embarrassed smile and turned with as much dignity as a man caught out could manage. As he left the office, he failed on his attempt not to stare at Celia. She wore white summer ankle pants and a brown blouse that hugged the sensual contours of her young body. Those were the last clothes Benoit would see her in for more than nine years.

*   *   *

Memory is crueler than history.

As Marco Valieri sat in the waiting room while his wife Celia went into surgery, he thought back to the first time he saw her. Not much of an orchestra fan, he'd been given a free ticket to the show and planned to cut out at intermission. He wound up staying past the last encore, unable to take his eyes off the girl in the third row. All women were worth one look, but Celia demanded many more. Innocence and beauty flowed out of her cello as if she channeled her essence into each note. The music wrapped around him. After the concert he waited thirty minutes outside of the Carnegie Hall stage door. They married eight months later in St. Anselm's.

Touring kept Celia away from Marco six months of the year. He felt like a newlywed even as they entered their third year of matrimony. As a

46

fashion photographer, his eyes blinked over quite a few stunning creatures. At the end of the day, it was only her face that filled the frame.

The minor surgery was supposed to be routine. Nothing to worry about. A small detour in the rear view mirror of their life together. As soon as he saw the doctor's face, he knew life would never be the same.

*　　*　　*

Benoit's work at the hospital became mundane. The dreary September Saturday after first seeing Celia Valieri, he journeyed twenty miles from the hospital to visit Tilden, a registered nurse he met while at medical school. They sat at a table in the second floor cafeteria of Sunny Day, a long-term care facility for the old, stroke-afflicted, and comatose. The building was cold both outside and in, but at least the dreary puke green walls were free of the offensive graffiti the neighborhood gangs painted on the soot-covered brick. The smack of a rock hitting the outside window startled both men.

"Gentrification can't happen fast enough for me," Tilden said as he turned away with disgust from the damaged window. "These goddamn hoodlums think this hospital is their enemy. Most of them will end up here one way or the other. All on the taxpayers' tab."

"They're kids," Benoit said. "Breaking windows is part of their job description."

Tilden shrugged. "I don't understand vandalism. Never did. Even as a kid."

Benoit considered the window. The rock's dent had unleashed a spider web of cracks. "Glass can shatter in so many different ways," he said. "Each crack leads to another crack and causes damage that spreads farther down the line. An infinite number of patterns only limited by the pane."

"Sounds like you've been sampling the meds chest again," said Tilden.

*　　*　　*

Marco couldn't understand it. Something in Celia's body reacted adversely to the anesthesia during her operation to remove an ovarian cist. Although the procedure was simple, she failed to respond to any pleas, both medical and emotional. They called her an *apallic* patient, which meant her eyes remained open even though she was lost in a coma.

"Surgery is not a science."

"There are always risks."

"It's in God's hands."

47

The doctors, oh so empathetic, espoused such nuggets of wisdom. That's why they made him sign those release forms, to exonerate the hospital from liability. Paper excuses were not going to stop Marco from blaming them for his wife's condition.

At first, he cried. Then shouted. He went through a myriad of emotions in direct contrast to his wife's blank existence. The first month he rationalized her absence as if she was out on tour. He visited every day to play her the music that used to flow out of her, hoping it could somehow seep into her body and nourish her soul back to the waking world. She continued to stare into a space he couldn't visit, the symphonies falling on ears made deaf by a cruel God.

Marco Valieri loved his wife. He vowed to stay by her until she woke up from the nightmare. The doctors lowered their eyes and slowly shook their heads.

"She is a vegetable."

"You should move on with your life."

"After this much time, it's unlikely she will ever regain consciousness."

He smoldered with anger as he stared at the haggard face in the mirror. Why should he build a new life when there had been no chance to finish the old one, like a concerto paused in the first movement? Living became a losing race that his wife couldn't even enter.

* * *

The first months were the most difficult. Watching. Passing by four or five times a day, sneaking a peek into the room to see the grounded angel. The doctor's chart was explicit. Although her body continued to function, her mind was a vegetable. No future or past, just a collection of tissue and skin, blood and brain. The world turned a different page each day while she remained a dead end story, a beautifully gilded book with no words inside. Or maybe just unreadable. In her coma, Celia could not see, smell, hear, speak, or think.

But that didn't bother Benoit.

He sneaked into the room just to gaze at her at first. She was so beautiful. As perfect as the first time he laid eyes on her. Her face still shined despite a lack of expression on her features. Her eyes gazed dully into space. The nurse on duty was lazy, allowing her exquisite lips to chap. He touched them once with a tentative finger and nearly jumped out of his own skin when the day nurse wandered in and destroyed the moment.

* * *

Marco's eye began to remain in the viewfinder of his camera a second or two after snapping the picture. His heart pumped blood just a little harder during certain shoots. With a yearning he both craved and feared, he began looking at one or two of his models with something more than professional appreciation.

Visits to the coma ward decreased to three times a week, then twice, then only on Sundays. He touched Celia less and less. The length of his stays also decreased as he sat with sullen face looking anywhere but at his wife. Bouquets of fresh flowers became single roses, then plastic.

When he chanced to look at her his depression deepened. Zero brain activity, the doctors said without looking him in the eyes. Her role in the movie of his life faded, as she became a secondary character left on the cutting room floor. His parents back in Argentina told him he must forget. In truth, it was getting even harder to remember. Their life together started to fade like the dreams they once had. One time he even shouted at her to wake up and collapsed onto the bed with his head buried in his hands.

*   *   *

When Celia moved into a long-term facility, Benoit followed her there, leaving his job as a hospital anesthesiologist to be reborn as a ward attendant at Sunny Day's long-term care facility. Night school classes enabled him to round out his medical training. Cosmetology went from a passing interest to degreed proficiency. He prided himself on being able to apply makeup better than most of the women in the ward. Nails and skin care proved easier to master than hair cutting. He eventually excelled in all. Tilden, the floor's supervising RN, approved his request to include Celia Valieri in his responsibilities.

Touching her for the first time as her primary caretaker was a revolution for his senses. Maybe he could produce the same electric spark inside of her, just for one moment. Enough sparks might one day create a flame to awaken her. It could take years. He was in no hurry. Love was the second hand on a clock, forever going around and around. The destination was in the journey.

*   *   *

Even sympathy has a shelf life. Marco learned pity was a burden better given than received. He drank heavily the night before his last visit to Celia. Alcohol was a great way of looking at everything and seeing nothing.

He stayed less than five minutes and didn't even kiss her goodbye as the orderly stood in the corner protectively waiting to change her bedpan.

He proposed to Ruth, an account executive for Chanel, three days after the two-year anniversary of Celia's arrival in the coma ward at Sunny Day.

* * *

Benoit lifted Celia's limp arm and dipped the sponge into the warm soapy water. With painstaking care he dabbed the underarm. She was due for a shave in a day or two. He liked to finish all the appendages before moving to her chest. He cupped the fleshy breast, as firm as it was that very first day they became intimate. He saved the nipple for last, being extra sensitive with the sponge. Her breasts would jiggle in time with the revolution of the drying towel on her flat stomach.

"The intravenous drip is the best diet plan a woman could hope for," he teased her.

He used a special chamois cloth for the vaginal area, dabbing at the brown tuft of pubic hair with the artistic delicacy of familiarity. Celia's period still happened with clockwork precision. Although her eyes stared at a point no living person could see, he always imagined she was looking up at him.

Trips around the ward. Outings for fresh air. Poetry readings at night. All these activities he approached and planned with the vigor of courtship. Her beauty still mesmerized him. Celia Valieri lived in a world with no beginning, middle, or end—a broken calendar with no seasons. She would love him soon enough.

* * *

As time dragged on, so did the malpractice lawsuit. The lawyers argued over the value of pain and suffering without ever feeling any of it. No amount of money could fill the void that was once Celia. No one could pinpoint fault. Medicine is not a science. Apparently, the legal system around it is. Marco couldn't handle the emotional cost of the proceedings. Twenty-eight years is too short a time to start looking back. Besides, he had a pregnant wife to consider.

"Just finish it," he told the lawyers.

* * *

"Why can't technology apply to the brain-dead?" Tilden asked Benoit. They sat in the break room having a cup of coffee to survive a long shift. "You know, somehow jump-start them like a car with a dead battery?"

Benoit shook his head at his colleague's stupidity. "That's why the computer will never replace man. There's no mathematical formula for the sparkle in a woman's eyes, the alluring way she can move her body, the timbre of her laugh, or the unreasonable nature of her mind."

"You got a new girlfriend?" Tilden asked before reverting to his theory. "I mean…we can resuscitate the heart. Hell, even replace it."

"We can fill it with blood, but not with love," Benoit said.

"You're right, there." Tilden downed his coffee and strolled out of the lounge.

Benoit sat alone for a long while to contemplate his predicament. He had tried to date other women, but none measured up. Celia was the only one for him. She carried no baggage and turned a blind eye to his shortcomings.

He wandered into her room and placed a hand to her chest. Her heart beat strong. Closing his eyes, he reassured himself he was doing everything to be in that heart.

"If we were smart," Benoit lamented to the darkness, "we wouldn't have a heart."

*   *   *

Marco and Ruth Valieri moved away from New York, across the country to San Francisco, the most European of American cities. The pending lawsuits were left behind with his first wife whose name he could not even bear to pronounce. Despite divorcing her, Celia's last name remained Valieri on all hospital records. For all intents and purposes, she only existed on paper.

*   *   *

"There is no grief like the grief that does not speak," Benoit read and then closed the book. He leaned over and kissed Celia on the forehead.

"You're reading poetry to her?" said a surprised voice from the crack in the door.

He turned to see Tilden's head peeking into the room lit by only the reading lamp bought at a garage sale. His reply was matter-of-fact. "Longfellow is her favorite."

Tilden rolled his eyes. "Longfellow, eh?"

"Come on in, but be quiet. She's sleeping."

51

Although Tilden wondered at the lunacy of his friend's delusions, he followed instructions and crept lightly into the room. "You give her ten times more attention than any other patient."

"I'm not working now." Benoit placed a tender hand on Celia's wrist. "This is my time. Our time."

"She's a vegetable, Ben. All the poetry in the world won't change that."

Benoit stood up and took an aggressive step towards Tilden. "There is life inside of her. I am inside of her."

Tilden took a step back, not sure how to interpret both his words and his intentions. "How long has she been here? Four years?"

"Five years, seven months and twenty-three days."

"Give it up, Ben. It's God's will."

Benoit cast a sour face in Tilden's direction. "Wills are what the dead leave behind for the living."

Tilden dipped his head in defeat. As he turned, he whispered, "I'll pray for you both."

Benoit held his reply until Tilden's muffled footsteps receded from the room.

"I don't believe God is listening."

*   *   *

Marco took his young son to the Natural History Museum during their first visit back to New York. Ricky Valieri gazed with awe at the artifacts encased in glass as he ran in figure eights around the cavernous rooms. The dioramas interested the boy the most. His fascinated face left greasy impressions on the glass before he scampered to the next diorama. A scene depicting Eskimos captivated him for a minute before he ran to see the American Indians sharpening arrowheads and weaving rugs.

Marco lingered at the Eskimo diorama, unable to take his gaze off the female mannequin with blue eyes and long, silky brown hair lying in a bed of sealskin and thick leather straps. The igloo centered in a field of white. A heavy fur blanket surrounded her like a shroud. He felt his head swim. He squeezed his eyes shut, but it was of no use. The image of Celia stabbed his heart like an ice pick. In tears he caught up to his son and hugged him until they both cried.

*   *   *

Celia woke up three days shy of her thirty-second birthday.

She lay naked on the bed like candy without the wrapper. Her breasts were still full with the resiliency of youth. During her sponge bath, Benoit clumsily spilled some lukewarm water over her pubic area. Surely the blink of her eyes was born of his imagination. The brittle sound escaping her throat made him jump back. Another blink. Then it happened. He stared wide-eyed, mouth slack and hands limp at his sides. The birth of a dream.

Her eyes swept over him like a blanket warming his soul. For the first time in their relationship, he was the shore and she the wave.

* * *

Marco Valieri was notified of Celia's miraculous recovery. He broke down and wept upon hearing the news, though whether they were tears of joy or sorrow he could not say. He refused to see his ex-wife, even phone her. What could they talk about? His two children with a third on the way? A daughter he hoped would look like his wife, Ruth? His guilt over the divorce papers he signed from his adopted home of Los Angeles, as she lay oblivious in a hospital room? The doctors offered no explanation for Celia's awakening aside from Divine Intervention. He bitterly wondered how much they charged for that and got roaring drunk.

* * *

Time had been fast-forwarded for Celia. She woke up to a world of lost years that were like the main story ripped from the center of a book. Nothing made any sense. The incarceration of sleep had stolen her life and dreams. Letting go of Marco and the life she was supposed to live took time and therapy, neither of which she much cared for. She couldn't play the cello anymore. Music no longer flowed through her fingers as it had before the coma. Inspiration had packed its bags and moved out.

"There is nothing holier, in this life of ours, than the first consciousness of love—the first fluttering of its silken wings," Benoit recited to her on their first proper date. "It's Longfellow."

Smiling had never been something foreign to her. Now she found herself forcing the expression. Benoit's devotion and dedication evoked feelings of gratitude, an emotion not fit to support a relationship. Eventually, she looked on him with appreciation that grew into affection.

Occasionally during lovemaking she tingled with a secret desire, a yearning for a feeling her body knew deep in its tissues which Benoit could not provide. She remained faithful to him and faithless to herself. A part of her longed to see Marco again, while another, more practical part resented his abandonment.

53

"Ye are better than all the ballads
That ever were sung or said;
For ye are living poems,
And all the rest are dead."

Celia closed the poetry book and looked up at Benoit. His smile was pert, forced. In his face was a disappointment neither could understand. She was still pretty, still had a voluptuous figure. But something was missing. Why did her touch no longer excite him?

He remembered seeing Celia over twelve years ago lying on a gurney in the generic white hospital smock. The nipples of her breasts playfully poked at the cotton robe. Her long hair was wrapped into a bun like a silk turban secured with safety pins. Long-lashed lids covering those beautiful blue eyes. Her lips so ripe and alluring.

For the first time in his life, he questioned his actions that day. He remembered picking up Celia's chart and viewing the section about allergies. The anesthesiologist assigned to her surgery wasn't at fault for her coma. The miracle was Benoit never got caught.

* * *

He saw her three days after All Saints Day, the Day of the Dead.

Snow frosted the ground, a calling card for an early winter. Cold air swirled around the hospital's entrance as old and young huddled inside to feel the heat seep into their arthritic hands and lives. Cars lined up to jettison the sick. The hospital was a breathing organism cursed to feed on sorrow, yet nourished by hope. Benoit had taken a position in the Anesthesiology Department after leaving Sunny Day Long Term care nearly a year ago.

She appeared out of the steam emanating from a sidewalk grate, dressed in black cotton pants and a thick suede coat lined with fur. Luckily Benoit had stopped by the pharmacy to buy some gum or he may have missed her. Her appearance resurrected his faith and patience. Maintaining a safe distance, he followed her into the obstetrician's office.

After signing in, Jessica Garberra shed her jacket and sat down with an old copy of *Newsweek*. Her blue angora sweater strived to contain her mellifluously curved body. Blond hair flowed down her shoulders like a golden waterfall. Twin emerald eyes hinted at the cache of preciousness her lips seemed to confirm. She sat next to a woman whose designer clothes bragged of superiority, but could not compete with Jessica's graceful presence. Her chair might as well have been a throne in the stifling waiting room. Certainly the gods paid attention when they cast her into his world.

Surgery is not a science. It is an art. If Van Gogh could have painted wheat fields or sunflowers with the passion this woman inspired, the artist would never have sacrificed an ear much less a life for love.

The world of the operating room is imperfect. Jessica Garberra was perfect.

Benoit had to have her.

Fire Escape

Using a fire truck for an escape vehicle was Eggars' idea. No one ever suspects that we're bank robbers driving away from the scene of a crime. Just crank up the siren and watch the vehicles pull over to make way. Those yellow jumpsuits make our faces disappear from people's memory. Think of a traffic accident. You could steal the hubcaps off a car rolling by at five miles per hour while the driver rubbernecks the scene. The best part is all of the people waving and giving us a thumbs-up as we pass by. It's like they're thanking us for stealing their money.

The five of us met at the Unemployment Office where a little man with no sympathy or jobs to hand out made us sign a bunch of forms without much hope for employment. I'm a paramedic. At least, I used to be. Made $48K a year working for the city. Took me two years of school, sixteen months working in an ambulance, and seven years of experience saving lives to get to that level. Despite the long hours, I loved the job. Something about helping people who could no longer help themselves appealed to me. One day erased all of that. They fired me and handed me a check for two weeks' severance and thank you very much but we don't need you anymore. I guess the recession caused a decline in people getting hurt.

Eggars runs one of those eBay places that doesn't really buy or sell things. Everything he brokers is stored in his warehouse, where we do our planning for the jobs. I've seen anything and everything in that place from a tooth that resembles the Virgin Mary to a U.S. Navy Hornet jet. They even sell real fire engines along with the parts to outfit them. So it doesn't look at all suspicious when we pull in through the big bay doors in the middle of the afternoon. The area is zoned for industrial use anyway, so there's not a lot of prying eyes. Even the clothes we use are from his place. Somewhere in Duluth some dude is wearing the Guess jeans we used in an armed robbery three weeks ago. I wonder if that makes him an accessory to the crime.

When I leave the warehouse I try to convince myself this is the last time. It's the fifth time I've lied to myself. Before I head home I stop at a bar for a couple of shots to dull my conscience. The wad of cash in my pocket is a powerful deceiver. It's just the smaller bills from the tellers' boxes. None of our crew ever uses the big money, the stuff from the vaults.

The plan is to sit on that for a couple of years. My stash is earmarked to pay for my kids to go to college someday, something an unemployed paramedic can't afford. None of us are looking to get rich; what with my mortgage and my kid brother's kidney operation I'm just trying to get by. I get less than the others since all I do is pull the false fire alarm in a nearby store to bottleneck the cops and real fire fighters while we all jump on our fire truck to make our getaway.

It's already twilight when I get home to my half of the duplex we share with a single mom who has fallen on hard times. My neighbor used to be a paralegal but now works the front counter of a chiropractor's office for minimum wage. She's got three young kids in grade school. When she has to work late I often invite them over for dinner or to hang out with my kids.

The front door isn't locked. That doesn't bother me, because there's nothing much to steal in our home. Dino, my seven year old, is watching Power Rangers on the television (it's an old tube model, not a flat screen) while Tess does her homework on the dining room table. They run over and give me a big hug when I barge into the living room. Rachel is in the kitchen. Smells like dinner is going to be fajitas again. You gotta love Mexican food because it's cheap and good for you. Lavish enough hot sauce on and it even tastes pretty good. I go into the kitchen to give my wife a perfunctory kiss. After eleven years our lives are a dance we perform without the need for music. Before dinner Dino and me head outside to play catch in the remaining light. After dinner I'll play a game with Tess and read to both of the kids before bed.

Once the kids are down and Rachel has cleaned up, I plop into my ratty old recliner and switch the tube to the local news. Rachel brings me a beer and sets down a cup of tea for herself. She sprawls out on the couch. The news plods on about all the bad things happening in the world. Someday, I wish they'd have a channel that only reported the good stuff, positive stories to make us feel good. Of course, if they ever did create such a channel, I couldn't get it because we no longer have cable.

Eight minutes into the ten o'clock news a picture of the Third National Bank appears on the screen. I try to feign indifference but I can't help but strain to hear what they're saying. The authorities report that three masked men armed with automatic weapons stormed the bank just after the lunch hour and made off with $52,000 in cash. The cops have no idea how the robbers got away from the scene of the crime. Rachel doesn't even lower the book she's reading. I finish my beer and head to the kitchen for one more.

When I come back her eyes are on the television, though her book is still propped up on her lap. The anchorman is talking to the City Fire Chief about the spate of false alarms that has besieged the city. They must have made the connection to the robberies, but haven't released it to the press. Sometimes I pull an alarm two or three days before the job, just to throw them off. On the screen, a picture of a guy in a hospital bed replaces the two men talking. Volunteer Tim Flannery fell off the back of a truck heading for one of the fake fires. He broke both legs and now cannot work his regular job. A collection is being taken to help him with his medical bills.

"It's terrible," Rachel says. "Kids pulling false alarms."

"How do you know its kids?" I ask.

Rachel is smart. Before she married me and started a family, she was going for her Masters in Biology. Her eyes swivel over to look at me. "Grown men shouldn't have time for such nonsense."

"How do you know its men and not women?"

Her shoulders collapse as if she's explaining something simple to an even simpler child. "Women consider how their actions affect others. Men are more narcissistic. The male machismo feeds itself while the female nurtures the species. It goes back to the cavemen. Club first and ask questions later."

"Is that a blatant generalization or scientific bigotry?"

"It's basic evolution," she says. "When a man sees a woman, he looks at her boobs and her hips. The two most important points of reproductive capacity. A woman looks deeper. She wants a provider."

"How did your opinion that men are more likely to pull false fire alarms than women turn into a conversation about Freud fucking Darwin?"

She gives me that look of disgust that I've seen all too often since I got laid off. Being a security guard at a mall–my current 'profession'–hasn't done much to bolster me in her eyes.

"Your crudeness merely corroborates my point." She turns her attention back to the book on her lap.

The cute weather girl with the big tits and the ample hips is on the screen by the time we finish our little discussion. She reports that we're in for a chance of thunderstorms over the next couple of days and that the pollen index should go down for asthma sufferers. I crack open my beer and sink half of it. The weather girl renews my faith in both Darwin and Freud.

*   *   *

Working security at the mall sucks. I hate my job. Every time I bust some kid shoplifting, I kind of feel guilty. The average age of these perps is getting older by the week. Just last Tuesday I nabbed a sixty-year-old woman trying to rip off socks and shoes from the Nike Store. Next day, I had to call the cops on some indigent woman straddling the escalator at Nordstrom's.

58

She literally dropped her drawers and started peeing into the mechanism. So much for Rachel's thesis on the evolution of man versus woman.

Eggars calls to tell me our next job is the Travelers Bank on Eighth Street. We meet on Saturday a week before the hit to go over the plans. I don't pay much attention to the bank part, as I'll be a block away in a sporting goods store pulling the diversionary fire alarm. As long as I know where Bronson will be with the fire truck to meet up, I'm good.

Friday comes at last and I'm itching for action. These little forays into crime energize me in some weird, middle-age crisis way. It's like I'm in some TV show and all I'm missing are super powers. First time I was nervous as hell. By the fourth one, I felt like I'd been doing it all of my life. The beautiful aspect is that even if we get busted, I'm not the one robbing the bank. I know intrinsically what I'm doing is wrong, but a man's got to live and take care of his family. No matter what the cost.

It's easy to get someone to cover for me at the mall. I tell Rachel that I may be home early today. She tells me "not to bother" because she's got the kids scheduled for a play date in the neighborhood with some single parent and his two sons. Something about a BBQ. She adds a half-hearted invitation to drop by.

The two-story Sports Authority store is crowded as the lunch hour nears. It's a stone's throw from the Travelers Bank where my cohorts are getting into position. With a constant eye on my watch, I rummage around the skiing section and check out some of the latest footwear along a full wall dedicated to shoes. The sneakers are all neon and straps and zippers. Whatever happened to good ol' black and white with laces?

Our crew has got it down to a science. By now the guns are out at the bank and the money is changing hands. In exactly three minutes I'm going to walk around the corner near the bathrooms and pull the fire alarm. I chose this location because there is no security camera in the area to film my little indiscretion. The thought of that poor volunteer fireman with the broken legs creeps into my head, and I have to banish it and remember that I'm doing this for my family. It's not my fault the economy forced my hand.

Everything goes according to plan. The siren starts to wail as I hurry out of the store with the rest of the patrons. I go down the street towards the idling red fire truck with Bronson at the wheel in his yellow outfit. As I climb aboard, I can see our three cohorts running towards us. Moments later we're pulling away from the curb with our siren blaring. Everyone is changing into his yellow jumpsuit. Eggars looks kind of frustrated. I get the feeling today's take is not what we were hoping for. Still, it being a Friday and all, the tellers' tills will be full and the useable portion of our cuts is all that really matters right now.

Just as we start to pick up speed I hear a horn blaring. The brakes lock and we're thrown off balance as the back end of our truck skids hard to the left. There is that awful screeching sound that seems to be suspended in time before the deafening crash. Metal crunches. I'm jolted forward into two of the other guys. There is that split second of silence before all hell breaks loose.

Eggars crawls out of the pile we've become. "What the hell, Bronson?"

"We broadsided an SUV," Bronson shouts from the fire truck's cab.

"We?" Eggars asks.

I peek over the side of the fire truck. Our front fender is toast. The van we've hit is shredded and on its side. We've almost ripped the thing in half. The engine is steaming and a smoky haze surrounds the downed vehicle. Bronson puts the fire engine in reverse to disengage from the SUV with a wrenching metallic groan. He backs up enough to be able to clear the damaged vehicle and shifts to first gear. Only then can I hear the cries from the crushed car. The distant sound of a siren signals the fire engine coming to the decoy call at the Sports Authority.

"Go, go, go!" Eggars manically waves his arm around. The other guys scramble to get their fireman outfits on.

"There's people hurt in there."

Eggars' hand freezes mid air and he looks at me strange. "What? Are you out of your mind? Get on your gear. We got to get as far from here as possible."

"What about those people?" I ask, pointing.

"You a paramedic or a bank robber?" one of the guys asks.

"What about them?" Eggars asks. "They'll be fine."

"You don't know that."

"What I know is that we're leaving." Eggars turns away from me. Before he ducks down, he shouts, "Bronson. Get it in gear and let's cruise. *Now.*"

Our fire truck starts to pull away from the scene of the accident. A kid that can't be more than ten-years-old crawls out of the wrecked metal. He looks like one of the boys from my son Dino's school. He's covered in blood and crying. There are other screams. I can decipher three different tones. There's a family dying in there.

The truck is going about ten mph when I start climbing down the ladder on the side and jump to the pavement. My left ankle takes most of the shock from the fall as I roll with my momentum. Ignoring the numerous cuts and scratches I hobble over to the SUV. Our fire truck pulls away with the siren delivering its false message. I notice the people on the street are frozen. Half of them look skeptically at the retreating fire truck. The other half stare with voyeuristic complacency at the tragic scene I am limping towards. Only a couple of Puerto Rican guys covered in tattoos dressed in wife beaters and blue jeans rush over to help the family.

The kid that I saw has a broken leg and a pretty bad cut. I get him laid out and have this woman keep pressure on his wound and make sure he stays put. By then, one of the Puerto Ricans has pulled out another kid, probably four or five years old. Poor thing is bawling his lungs out. His face is covered in blood. I tell the Puerto Rican I'm a paramedic. He nods once and leaves the kid with me while he goes to rescue another member of the family.

The youngster may have internal bleeding. I check him over and do what I can, which isn't much. I scream for someone to call 911, hoping the paramedics the city didn't fire are on their way with some much-needed medical equipment. Poor kid—he's alone and scared and wondering what the hell happened. I can't even imagine one of mine going through something this traumatic. When I look up, the two Puerto Rican guys are dragging this old lady along the pavement. One of them signals with his other hand by pounding his chest. I understand him loud and clear.

CPR on a woman of her apparent age is tricky. I don't want to hurt her but I've got to get her breathing again. First thing is to make sure she hasn't choked on her tongue. After clearing the passage, I lightly apply pressure on her chest. Nothing. Another try gets the same lack of results. Mouth to mouth will hopefully do the trick. As I bend over her, the sounds of police sirens join in with the fire truck that must be at the false alarm by now. My only focus is the woman I'm about to breathe life into.

I hold her nose and breathe into her mouth. Nothing. I try again. Red and blue lights are flashing in front of me. I fill her lungs up again. Finally, a cough and a pulse. I've pulled another life back from the brink. Just like when I did this sixty hours a week. It feels good, like I've washed away a disguise and can see myself in the mirror again. I look up as a wave of people rush towards me. A paramedic I don't recognize nudges me out of the way without even a word of thanks.

I need to get out of here, which is no longer going to be easy. Fortunately, I'm still in my street clothes and not my fireman's costume. My skin is slick with sweat and there's some blood on my clothing. The rest of my crew is long gone and my car is at Eggars' warehouse. Even if I find a way back, there's no telling what kind of reception I'll get. Or whether they'll even give me my take. Which makes me feel both vindicated in my complicity in this accident and resentful of their lack of concern.

On the other hand, my presence here is the perfect alibi. There's a good chance the police will be able to track down the fire truck because of the accident. Perhaps they'll finally make the connection that will lead to

Eggars' place. To hope he'll do the honorable thing and not sell the rest of us out is preposterous. If no one saw me jump off the fire truck I've got a shot of getting out of this mess.

The cops detain me for their report. Forty-five minutes later the family has been whisked away in ambulances. The damaged SUV has been moved to the side of the road. The tow truck driver is shaking his head as he secures the scrap metal onto the bed of his truck for transportation to some junkyard. A cop has a broken bumper piece in his hand as he speaks with a couple of other officers. Even from here I can see the red paint from our fire engine on the scrap. They also have a cracked front light and other pieces that didn't come from the SUV. Not to mention countless witnesses, some of who might have seen me jump from the truck.

As I give my statement to the police, I half expect one of them to slap a pair of handcuffs on me. After signing their paperwork and giving contact information, they tell me I'm free to go. I get a good amount of thanks and back slaps. As I turn to leave, a couple of reporters converge on me to speak to today's hero, the lone bright spot for this evening's news. A few congratulatory comments later I break through the small crowd that still remains. It's absurd—all those years I helped people as a paramedic and rarely even received a 'thank you'. Here I am aiding people hurt in an accident while robbing a bank and suddenly I'm six o'clock news fodder.

The bus system gets me within six blocks of my house. Tomorrow I'll go retrieve my car and find out if Eggars is going to ball me out or give me my cut. The walk home makes me realize how spent I really am, especially with my sprained ankle from jumping off the fire truck. My clothes are filthy and reek of something I can't begin to categorize. Smoke, sweat, blood. My thoughts veer towards the amount of money that woman's life cost me. For the first time I can quantify what a life is worth. To me, at least.

I'm three blocks from home when I smell it. Someone must be burning trash. Another block and I see the dissipating plumes of smoke. The acrid air is stifling in this heat. Before I know it, I'm trotting and picking up speed. Turning the corner, I see the line of police cars and two ambulances. The scene stops me dead in my tracks. The paramedics' lack of urgency reveals the futility of their efforts. The rotating red emergency lights moves in slow motion.

It's not my house, but something in my gut tugs at me. Each step reverberates through my body. My heart is pounding. My mouth is dry. When I reach the yellow police tapeline Jerry Colangelo, a paramedic I did shifts with when I shared his job title, meets me. His eyes burn into mine. Before he even opens his mouth, my stomach tenses and I feel sick. The hand on my shoulder is a hundred pound weight.

The voice isn't mine, but it comes from deep in my throat. "Talk to me."

"Rachel is already on her way to the hospital. I think she'll be okay."

"Rachel? My wife? What's she doing here?"

"I thought you...?" Jerry looks down and away. He swallows hard before bracing himself to look into my searching eyes. "She was visiting. The fire...it looks like it started outside the house...probably the old grill on the porch. Maybe the kids were playing with the starter..."

"Kids? What kids?" My head darts around the yard. In the street are three black body bags. They're so small...

He pries my grasping hands from his arms and takes a deep breath. "Dino and Tess. They were playing with..." His eyes roll upward as he searches his mind for information. "The older boy...Benjamin? The blast...something ignited..." He can't finish his sentences, not while looking at me.

I'm on my knees. My eyes are tearing and it's not from the smoke.

He stares down at me with pity. I know the look. How many brothers and sisters, friends and neighbors, husbands and wives did I look upon with that same benevolent stare of the powerless?

"We did all we could to...the fire...it caught so quickly. The woodpile out back...caught inside...damn fire truck...if only it could have...just a few minutes sooner..."

A poison has been unleashed in my bloodstream. My head is swimming. "I want to see them..." I try to push away from him and stagger toward the burnt out house. "Tess? Where are you, baby?" Blind with tears and desperation I call into the dark emptiness. "Dino?"

"I'm sorry," is all Jerry can say. "Goddamn fire truck..."

My eyes close. The fire inside of me has been extinguished as I crumple to the pavement. The fire truck that would have answered the alarm at the neighbor's house was late because it was busy checking a false alarm. The alarm I initiated. My kids are dead. Budget cuts, the economy, the city, Rachel, my neighbor—none of them are at fault. It's me. And no amount of money is ever going to make things right again.

Man As Beast

"How long you been on Death Row?" asked Maynes.

Cozy snorted and walked a circle in the cage that had been home since execution loomed as his future. "Six weeks." He shook his head. "If they're going to do it, I wish they'd just get it over with. Waiting is a slow, cruel death."

"Ha!" Maynes spat out the word. "They wrote the book on cruel."

Cozy couldn't see Maynes, but he knew about him. For about seven years, all anybody in the drug business heard about was how good Maynes was. "You had a good run."

"Yeah, I did." Maynes sneezed, what was left of his nasal canals feeling like sandpaper. Most of his septum had been eaten away by the cocaine. "You train yourself to be drawn to the stuff. Next thing you know…" His voice trailed off. "How long were you in the game?"

"About four years." Cozy scratched behind his ear, an affectation he couldn't remember acquiring.

"At first, it's quite a rush, isn't it?"

"I think it liked me more than I liked it." Cozy looked through the bars from a perspective he never imagined having.

"It's elusive, like trying to catch a train that never pulls into the station. You can keep up for a while, but eventually it just pulls away from you."

Cozy coughed. He was hungry. He remembered the early days and being actively recruited by the Drug Enforcement Agency. It was all swank meals and plush digs back then. They groomed him for the big time. But when he got too good at the game, they abandoned him like a bad habit, which is what he ended up with.

"You know," said Maynes, "we met before. When you were just getting started."

Cozy ducked his head. "I remember."

"I tried to warn you about how coke would consume you. 'Not me,' you barked back at me. 'I got it licked.' You were pretty sure of yourself."

The thought shamed Cozy.

64

"They all say that. Even me." Maynes hacked like a lifelong smoker. "You steal a bump here, a bump there. Next thing you now, it's stolen your soul."

"And you wind up here."

"And you wind up here," Maynes echoed.

A door down the hall opened and closed with a metallic clank. Soled shoes clicked closer and closer. The time had come for one of them to die.

Maynes closed his eyes at the sound of keys fumbling in a lock. A door opened. He raised his head and looked up. They weren't coming for him. Yet. He heard a whimpering noise next door and knew Cozy was being dragged to execution. He turned away, unable to bear the sight of a former DEA agent like himself disgraced.

The sound of the footsteps receded down the hall, punctuated by the slam of the metal door. Maynes was left with his thoughts. The drug had decimated his once strong and proud body. He curled up in the corner of his cell and thought about the things he'd done in his life, and the things he'd never get to do.

Death was a cruel lesson. The government in their hypocritical fight against drugs had forgotten one basic element: Drugs didn't kill; it was the lack of hope that killed. The drugs just made the passage easier.

He jerked at the sound of the door at the end of the hall clanging open. Cozy was gone, a soul passing without notice. It was his turn.

His faculties deserted him. He pissed on the floor as the cell door opened. A man came in and attached a metal wire to his collar. His legs ceased to work. The man had to drag him out of the cage, his claws scraping at the floor and finding no purchase. Maynes barked in protest, but his plea fell on deaf ears. His paws went limp as the executioner's lackey pulled him down the hallway, the hair on his once luxurious coat collecting dust from the tiled floor.

Men were nowhere near as honorable as dogs like him and Cozy.

Lost & Found

The Witness Protection Program had gone from being a Godsend to a death sentence for Sam Billings. Seven years ago the FBI swept his history clean. Although he and his family were safe, the prison of life in a small town in the northeast seemed a far crueler punishment than incarceration. He itched to pull one more job, plan one more heist, place one more bet, rather than blend in the 9-to-5 suburban hell that was Calder, Vermont.

Relocation meant driving an unpretentious car and staying within the speed limit while driving back and forth from his job at Bargain City Hardware. It meant going to a high school basketball game to watch Tommy score five measly points and grab three rebounds. It meant screening nineteen-year-old lotharios making plays for his seventeen-going-on-twenty-five-year-old daughter Marla. Or listening to his youngest Tricia bitch about Vermont being so much colder than Texas. A night out for him and Jean was a trip to the Ponderosa for the Cattle Driver Special instead of filet mignon at the Morton's in Dallas. What did the federal agents tell him? Don't make waves; still waters merely reflect. In other words, be everything he spent his life trying to avoid.

That damn Jimenez job did him in. Jerry Jimenez, the Texas Toad, ran heroin and prostitution out of his nightclub. The guy was skimming money, so they had to make an example of what happens to those who buck the system. Unfortunately, Jimenez ratted out to the Feds before Sam could get to him. There was a messy shootout. Sam and the tall Fed–Schiller was his name–were the last ones standing. Two of Sam's men were wounded and writhing on the pier. Schiller shot both of them dead and pointed the gun at him. The guy let him live on one condition–that Sam turn state's evidence. What else could he do? Oh, yeah. Did he forget to mention that the gun Schiller used to knock off two Zambrano Family soldiers on that dock was his? If he didn't talk, the Feds were going to make sure he died in a hail of bullets from his former employers before he got a chance to rot in jail. So he sang loud and clear. The contract on his life and his family still stood. No statute of limitations on vendettas.

*   *   *

Rick Tuffle lived at 715 Wilde Lane. All of the suburban streets in Calder seemed to be named after poets and writers, such as Dickens Way and Goetthe Avenue, which no native could pronounce correctly. The tree lined sidewalks and cookie-cutter houses radiated Stepford sameness. The scarcity of chain stores was replaced in the walking mall with used bookstores, antique shops, and coffeehouses, even a homemade ice cream parlor. The banks and major industrial companies had to sneak in wherever they could find a spot. He loved it.

Rick arrived in Vermont eleven years ago. A quiet, diminutive little man, he pretty much kept to himself. He looked like what he had become: a bookworm. His store, the Book's End, was nestled on Dante Corner off of Copernicus Square. The shop was a hodgepodge of used paperbacks and hardcovers arranged as if by a hurricane. The only things he cherished more than his books were his coins. Those, or course, weren't for sale. They were his passion. Most people had never heard of or seen the Eagle half-dollars, seated Liberty dimes, Fugio cents, or silver three-cent piece he cherished. No one knew about his impressive collection—not even collectors—until the newspaper article.

The *Vermont News* did a big story on his unique coins. There were two pictures accompanying the article. Rick refused to let them use his image. The first showed one of his fabulous Morgan dollars next to a Walking Liberty quarter and a three dollar gold piece. The second shot was of an 1838-O reeded edge Half Dol—the main impetus for the article. A New Orleans chief coiner stated that only twenty such half-dollar coins were struck. In an auction back in 1973, one coin fetched a price of $41,000. Current estimates ranged into six figures.

Even though the 1838-O was his most impressive and expensive coin it was not the nearest to his heart. That distinction belonged to a 1694 Carolina Elephant Token. The rare token's face was that of an elephant. The back read "God Preserve Carolina and the Lord's Proprietors". The tokens were struck in England as an advertising stunt to induce interest in the Carolina Plantation nearly a hundred years prior to the Declaration of Independence. Although Rick was born and raised in South Carolina, he hadn't been back in nearly twenty years. He missed the South dearly, and the Carolina Elephant token was a constant reminder of home.

*   *   *

Agent Schiller sipped his coffee and flipped through his magazine. Half of the 'Girls of the Southwest Conference' looked better than Miss September. The knock on his office door caused him to open a file folder and stick it on top of his desk. With mild annoyance he invited the visitor into his office.

"Hey, Steve," said Agent Vincent, his boss. "Did you get that last memo from HQ? About keeping tabs on cases?"

Schiller picked up a sheet of paper. With creased eyebrows he feigned inspection. It was a Xerox of the day's specials in the cafeteria. "Uh, let me see…"

"You know, about going from variable checks to a more regular system?"

"Oh, yeah. Yeah." He put the menu face down so as not to embarrass an Economics major that was a junior at Baylor. "What about it?"

"You call Billings lately?"

"Billings…Billings…" He searched his desk, opening a few folders and shuffling papers around his IN box. "Refresh my memory."

"The Jimenez job. The Zambrano goon you shipped off to Bumfuck, Vermont? Renamed him Sam Billings?"

"Sam Billings…" He rearranged more paperwork on his desk. "I saw it just this morning…gotta be here somewhere…"

Vincent shifted his weight and exhaled impatiently. "Try to handle that soon and log it in, will ya?" His eyes scanned the cluttered desk. "Jeez, you ever heard of a computer?"

"Yeah, I'll get right on that. Sorry, Angelo. I know it's here somewhere. I'm just so slammed right now…"

"Can't believe I need to remind you about him," Vincent said as he turned to leave. "After what happened…" He closed the door behind him.

Oh, he remembered, all right. Sam Billings was embedded on his radar. Not a day went by he didn't go over his plans for the bastard.

*   *   *

Sam Billings remembered the day he saw the article with the picture of the old coin from 1838. The one with the eagle clutching olive branches in one claw and arrows in the other. The bird looked like it was about to fly right off of the coin. What really caught his eye about the "half dol" was its estimated worth. Somewhere in the neighborhood of $100,000.

The article mentioned the owner's name but didn't have a picture of him. When it came to one-horse towns, Calder was just a pony. Finding the local who owned the coin didn't entail much effort. The man in question was a timid little man that reminded him of a bird that had fallen out of its nest. Easy prey for a big dog like himself.

He was thinking about the coin while drinking crap beer on Friday at the Loose Moose Saloon. The circle of peers he'd adopted to maintain his 'normal' identity hunkered down at their regular table with pitchers of Budweiser. The month of September meant local talk centered on the New England Patriots, the football team most Vermont residents adopted. Everyone had an opinion except him.

"I never liked Tom Brady," said Jim Durney, the mechanic from the gas station. "Anyone who would pose for the cover of a women's magazine like *GQ* shouldn't be helming a football team."

"*GQ*'s a men's magazine," said Tom Jeppeson.

"Hey, Brady took us to the Promised Land," Pete Jeppeson said. The Jeppesons looked like twin lumberjacks. "Three times."

"That was then," said bank manager Will Lester.

"At least we beat the Cowboys," said Jim Durney. "I hate the Cowboys."

Sam raised his glass with the others as he seethed inside. It felt like a lifetime ago when he was sitting in a luxury box sipping champagne with the owners watching Dallas win back-to-back Super Bowls. What could he possibly share with these guys? All they did was talk about their mundane lives. He had to drink twice as much beer so he could stomach them.

"I gotta take a leak." Sam slid out from the table. He walked past the row of booths against the wall and around the 'L' shaped bar where a few younger men and women sat sampling various brands of the saloon's microbrews. He salivated at the bottle of single malt scotch behind the bar. In his glory days, people used to bring him expensive bottles just to say 'hello' to him. Now, he had to stay away from the stuff. Can't be too careful...he hated himself for even thinking like one of those damn Feds.

Before hitting the bathroom he stepped outside onto the porch to grab some fresh air. As he stood there watching the traffic plod by, he noticed a little man walking past with head down. If it wasn't for the clothes and thinning hair, he could have been a little kid searching for pennies in the sidewalk cracks. A woman pushing a baby stroller passed the man and greeted him with a friendly, "Good evening, Mr. Tuffle."

It was him. The coin guy.

After hitting the bathroom, he returned to the table. The football chatter had given way to the best method for resurfacing your driveway. He wanted to pull a gun out of his pocket and shoot every last one of them dead. Of course, he didn't have a gun. Not anymore. He wanted to tell these mooks how much concrete you needed to sink a human weighing two hundred pounds and the amount of time needed for it to harden properly. He chewed on his lower lip and chugged more beer.

It was at that moment he decided to rob Rick Tuffle of his precious coin.

Rick kept his coin collection in the antique armoire in the living room. Calder being such a small town, he didn't feel it necessary to waste money on such precautionary measures as locks or security systems. Crime was limited to occasional acts of vandalism by the local teenagers. MARY LOVES DREW in black spray paint on the sandblasted concrete walls of the high school. Speeding tickets and the occasional drunken brawl at the Loose Moose. Toilet paper in the trees around Halloween.

The 1838-O, like most of its peers, was nestled in black velvet in its own clasped plastic case. Unlike the other coins, the Carolina Elephant resided in a sterling silver rectangular case with an inlaid art deco pattern of thick and thin lines. At least once a week, he lovingly extracted the coin from its perch of honor amongst the others and retired to the old chair by the front bay window. He sat with the coin on his lap for hours, letting it breathe the air with him as he reminisced about his youth. Hunting with his father. Stalking deer with his crossbow. Playing war games with BB guns. Shooting cans off of the fence until he got so good that he was a better shot than his dad, who served in Vietnam.

Then his dad died. Rick was only seventeen. Good thing the military took him in. No one thought a wimpy kid like him could handle it, but six years of being a Marine revealed otherwise. As he often said to people at his bookshop, "never judge a book by its cover." Even during his tour of duty he preferred to be left alone. Not many witnessed his short temper. Getting him angry was a very bad idea.

* * *

Agent Schiller flicked off the Patriots football game and retreated to his home office with a half-full bottle of beer. After a few keystrokes on his computer the Internet provided him with a copy of *The Calder Daily Reader*. He skimmed the articles. Most were of local interest with only a smattering of what was happening in the 'real' world. Seemed like the little Vermont town purposely avoided knowing about the war in Iraq, the President's struggles with Congress, or the state of the economy. Calder was one insulated town, kind of like 'Mayberry' in color.

Nothing like the city of Dallas, a city where both the best and worst of the world collided. His mind wandered back to a time when his wife was alive. She loved the pace of the city and refused to leave, despite his desire to move up the chain. The move to DC was precipitated by her death. A case of good tangling with evil and spitting out the innocent. He downed the remainder of his beer and repressed the desire to hurl the bottle across the room.

He wished he had pulled the trigger and blown Sam Billings' head off all those years ago. The little pissant should have been sent to prison for life at the very least. But, no, after he squealed on his mob brothers the FBI gave him a brand new life, all nice and polished.

Could they do that for him when his wife died at the hands of those bastards? No, of course not. All he got was condolences. Her death would prevent other innocent people from suffering the same fate because of the Zambrano Family. Well, that wasn't enough.

Calder would be Sam Billings' prison. He knew the man would eventually break out of the constraints of the small town, especially if nudged.

*   *   *

Breaking the rules always felt good to Sam. The 1838-0 coin lived only three blocks away, and it could fit into his pocket. What was that coin worth these days? Fencing it was out of the question. Too much risk to his family and identity. But this wasn't about money. This was about the actual job. Maybe he'd just stick it into a soda machine and buy himself a $100,000 Coke.

Tuffle seemed such an insignificant man, like the little fish you throw back into the pond even if you spent all day to catch him. Sam hated weak people.

The surveillance of Tuffle's house was exhilarating. Wednesday nights Tuffle walked to a sporting goods store on Joyce Way and then stopped at Brewer's Choice for an espresso on the way home. A round-trip of ninety minutes. More than enough time to get in the house, find the coin, and get back out. He started counting the days until the job.

*   *   *

Rick looked forward to the Wednesday junkets to Billy's Sporting Goods store. He'd make a beeline to the back counter where they kept the firearms locked with INVENTORY CONTROL tags attached to the trigger guards. Just the sight of the green and yellow Remington bullet boxes stacked neatly against the wall had a comforting effect on him. Although the selection was minimal, you could purchase a Leupold scope to increase accuracy on the Beretta Silver Pigeon .20 gauge or a Browning B425 Plus Sporter .12 gauge with the 30" barrel. He only browsed, because he could never buy a gun. That would require background checks.

71

At least he had his Sunday excursions in the woods. While most of Calder prayed to their God at church, he reveled in target practice. There was something fulfilling about splitting a leaf in half at two hundred feet or knocking an apple off the branch.

*　*　*

Agent Schiller couldn't postpone his phone call to Sam Billings much longer. Vincent was breathing down his neck and wanted the file updated. Billings' restlessness had to be overwhelming him by now. For seven years the bastard had resisted the temptation of crime. The few favors requested in their phone conversations had been categorically denied. Usually, he'd grant minor requests to the relocated witnesses—a hunting rifle here or a sports car there. But not Billings. That animal had to remain in its cage until it had no alternative but to try and break out.

*　*　*

Sam felt an almost orgasmic delight as his hands maneuvered the picks. The click of the tumblers falling into place was sweeter than a woman's moan. He pushed open the backdoor to Rick Tuffle's house and stepped inside.

Flicking on his Mag-Lite, he walked through the kitchen and into the living room. The same contractor built all of the houses on Wilde Lane, so the Tuffle's floor plan matched his home. There was a little den off the living room. This he searched first. Cluttered with old paperbacks, there was nothing of interest. No pictures on the wall or desk or the usual nick-knacks of a life where most of the road lay in the rear view mirror. Inside the desk were pencils and pens but no files or documents of personal interest. He checked his watch to make sure he didn't dally too long and went back into the living room. The thin flashlight beam crawled around the room, passing over the austere furniture, the old tube television, a large wooden armoire. A reflective glint from inside the armoire drew his interest. Stepping closer, he saw the numerous cases inside. Bingo.

The armoire wasn't locked. A bit disappointed at the ease of entry, he stood back to take in the shelves. He ran the flashlight along the six levels of coinage. The lower shelves were used as storage for coins in blue collector books. The cases got bigger and more spread out as his gaze went higher. Like liquor at a bar, the top shelf housed the best stuff. There were silver dollars with Greek heads in profile; Indian heads with full plumage; old quarters, dimes and nickels with busty, overweight women or eagles in assorted degrees of flight. E. Pluribus Unum. In God We Trust. Amen.

And then he saw it.

The most impressive case was silver with an inlaid pattern. Only one coin could command such extravagance, a coin probably worth more than the house itself. The 1838-O Half Dol. Feeling like he was abducting the king right in front of Parliament and the royal guards, he reached in and snatched the case from its place at the center of the top shelf. With the prize firmly in his grasp, he closed the armoire and locked it.

Ten minutes later Sam sat in the privacy of his study at home. When he opened up the case, the frowned. Something was wrong. He fished out the article from his desk with the picture of the 1838-0 Half Dol. The coin in the picture didn't look like the one in the silver case, not even close. He sat back in his chair and had a hearty laugh, flipping the coin up in the air. "Tails" he called as the coin bounced to the ground and eventually stopped gyrating.

The coin landed with the elephant side up.

* * *

Rick Tuffle tugged at the armoire and stepped back in surprise. He tugged a little harder, nearly pulling it away from the wall. It took him twenty minutes to find the key to unlock it. When he finally got it opened, he exuded a silent scream when he realized what had happened.

* * *

The Friday drinking session was in full swing. Sam felt so alive he bought the first two pitchers of Bud and treated himself to a shot of top shelf single malt. The Jeppesons were arguing with Jim Durney and Will Lester about the Patriots' three game losing streak. Sam sat back and contentedly stared at the ceiling. Still flying high over his violation of Tuffle's coin collection, he savored the current plan to go back and locate the 1838 coin. It might happen next week or next year. Didn't matter.

His reverie was broken by a sudden stoppage in the group's conversation. Mugs of beer were suspended between the table and mouths. Standing five feet from them was Rick Tuffle. The little man stared accusingly, unwaveringly at Sam.

Sam felt a cold rush go over his body. It wasn't a physical fear. In a fight, he figured he could rip Tuffle to shreds without spilling any of his beer in the process. It was something about that look. The little man's cold, unwavering eyes. Sam shouldn't have glared back, but he couldn't help himself. His mouth turned up in a defiant smirk. Tuffle's nod was barely perceptible before he turned and shuffled out of the Loose Moose Saloon.

73

"What the fuck was that all about?" said Jim Durney, wiping his clean hands on his dirty mechanic overalls.

"Beats the hell out of me," said Sam.

"He's a strange one," said Pete Jeppeson.

"Weirdest guy in town since he moved here," said Tom Jeppeson.

"About as aggressive as a sheep," said Durney.

"They fuck sheep over in New Zealand," said Will Lester. "Where men are men, and sheep are scared."

The table erupted in laughter. All but Sam. He took a pensive sip of his beer and didn't have anything to say the rest of the night. He couldn't shake that look Tuffle had given him.

* * *

Schiller hung up the phone and sat back in his chair. The Billings folder sat open and the man's face glared at him. A former Zambrano Family Mafioso with an arrogant smirk that made him want to ram his pen straight between the eyes. He wondered how the man looked now after seven years in Calder. Their conversation had been short, just a quick check on how he was getting on and if there were any problems. Usually, Billings would whine and complain. But, not this time. The smugness had returned to his voice, the swagger to his attitude.

He placed both elbows on his desk and buried his face in his hands. Closing his eyes he allowed himself to think about his dead wife. How they'd lay in bed an extra five minutes after the alarms went off, the warmth from her body making him sweat while she professed to feeling cold. Or how she would never let any food on her plate mingle; everything had to be separated. The way her crazy hair would always fall over her left eye. All that had been taken away and more when a stray bullet from Sam Billings' gun caught her during a hit on a rival Family member outside the bookshop where she worked in a Dallas suburb.

Schiller took a deep breath and let the memories of his wife evaporate. She stared back at him from the picture on his desk. A wave of love warmed his body and he smiled at her. When the smile faded he prepared the folder to be forwarded to Agent Vincent with a recommendation that Billings be relocated again. He decided to hold back the report just a little longer. Maybe, just maybe, he'd crack before they relocated him again. And if he did, perhaps the Zambrano Family might just find out who and where Sam Billings was. Funny how some information leaked out.

* * *

74

It had been a week since the theft, and five days since Tuffle's strange appearance at the Loose Moose. Sam was at home watching TV, the entire house to himself. Tommy was at an away basketball game. Jean had escorted Tricia to some mother-daughter extravaganza at school. And Marla was out gallivanting with some guy from the college football team who drove an old Cadillac. Bowl of popcorn sitting on his lap, he leaned back to watch Bruce Willis kick the crap out of some foreign guy when the picture went haywire.

Damn satellite cable. He trudged down the hall to the kitchen to get another beer. When he got back the living room was dark. He leaned over to check the end table lamp to see if the bulb blew since the TV was still spitting interference.

"Leave it off."

The voice was firm and steady. Sam jerked upright and turned to see Rick Tuffle in the corner of his living room.

"What the fuck are you doing in my house?" Sam said.

"The same thing you were doing in mine."

"What the hell are you talking about?"

"Don't be coy with me. I warn you."

"You warn *me*? In my own *goddamn house*? You fucking little worm..." Sam clenched his fists and stormed around the couch towards Tuffle.

Tuffle opened his overcoat to reveal a sleek automatic pistol. Sam froze and narrowed his eyes at the gun.

"You should be impressed," Tuffle said, seeing the recognition in Sam's face. "It's a Browning M1935 Hi-Power single action. Always my favorite."

"Your favorite?"

"Speaking of favorites, I'd like it back."

"Like what back?"

"Cut the crap." Tuffle took a menacing step forward. "You know why I'm here."

"You don't know who you're messing with, buddy."

Tuffle reached into his overcoat breast pocket and pulled out a dark greenish folder. Keeping the gun leveled all the while he threw the dossier onto the coffee table in front of Sam. The Browning looked surprisingly comfortable in Tuffle's hand. Like it belonged there.

"Read it."

Sam picked up the file. Inside was the picture of a man resembling Rick Tuffle. The differences were insignificant. The hair in the picture was dark and covered more of his head. There was a mustache, but the eyes were the same. Those beady little eyes. On the other side of the opened folder was a sheet that looked like an application. Upon further perusal, he discovered it was a fact sheet. With an FBI letterhead. It listed a name, Robert Peluso, and gave the height, weight, and the general description that fit Rick Tuffle. The physical information was followed by a list, a rap sheet:

Terminated: John Sargent, 4/23/82, Sector D-9, gunshot. Contract fulfilled.
Terminated: Sergio Delavane, 6/12/82, Mexico, gunshot. Contract fulfilled.
Terminated: Paul Wheeler, 9/9/82, Washington, gunshot. Contract fulfilled.
Terminated: Helen Prentice, 11/16/82, Manchester, UK, gunshot. Contract fulfilled.

And on it went. Three full pages listing what Sam knew were murders. Government hits on names from the underworld, political figures and military men. Years and years of death. The history of killing ended in October of 2005.

Sam slowly raised his head, his lips parting but unable to form a word.

"Not a bad resume, wouldn't you say?" Tuffle smiled for the first time.

"Who the hell are you?"

"I'm a fictional character, just like you."

A cold chill climbed up Sam's back. "It...can't be..."

"You think you're the only one?"

Sam shook his head back and forth helplessly.

"You broke the rules," Tuffle said. "You stole my past from me."

"You can have the coin back." Sam's voice was failing. His body sagged as he recognized the dead look in Tuffle's eyes. It was the same unyielding face others had seen so many times in the past when the gun was in his hand. The look that said you weren't going to walk away from this.

Tuffle's face didn't flinch as he pulled the trigger.

*   *   *

Agent Schiller sat in his office with *The Calder Daily Reader*. Splashed across the front page was a picture of Sam Billings with the tagline, 'Local Clerk Murdered'. What the article didn't mention was the Browning M1935 slug recovered from the dead man's body. Speculation ran rampant at the

FBI that the death reeked of a Zambrano Family hit. Which was why he was ordered to relocate the rest of the 'Billings' family ASAP.

The FBI knew about Rick Tuffle's past. What they didn't know about were the little favors that Tuffle's case manager, one Agent Schiller, had not only allowed, but also neglected to report. Certain anonymous packages sent to Tuffle, such as a Browning M1935 and other 'toys' for the man to play with.

He knew just where to relocate the Billings family. The town of Healy, Alaska, population 1,000 would be an ideal haven. For the past thirteen years Lance Kenderling, a politician's son and serial pedophile that the FBI had been compelled to help 'disappear,' had been living uneventfully in Healy. Kenderling liked kids the ages of Sam Billings' daughter.

No, he was far from through with the Billings family.

Ring Worm

The first punch lands square on my jaw. I roll with it, so it don't rattle me too much. Covering up, the next flurry only lands glove. Finding no flesh, he works on my stomach. Jabs and the occasional uppercut. He's a good puncher. I already knew that. It's just the first round, so he's trying to make a statement. Show me I'm in for a long, painful fight. He don't know the half of it. He's fighting for the money and the win. I'm fightin' for a hell of a lot more.

Back to my corner for a minute break. The crowd is just getting warmed up. So am I. I can't see past the first couple of rows for all of the lights they got splashed into the ring. My trainer is squawking in my ear, but I ain't listenin'. The energy around the ring is a mainline that flows through my veins until it reaches my fingertips and toes. C'mon, ring that goddamn bell. Round two is gonna be a little different. I'm gonna introduce Robbins to my right jab. Get'em real acquainted before Mr. Left Hook joins the party.

Robbins is a big, white middleweight. Weighed in at one-fifty-eight. He's got me by a few pounds, but I got the reach on him. That's why he comes at me like a bull, leading the charge with that Mohawk covered skull behind his gloves and tucked down to his chest. Seventeen fights, sixteen wins, twelve knockouts. Boy's got promise. If he can get past me.

Ding!

Round two. Robbins keeps charging at me, but I do a little more dancin'. Piss him off by pushing away his head with an open glove, flattening that spike of hair he's got. He rolls his neck around as he backs off. I can smell his sweat mixed with the cheap cologne they keep in them industrial-sized bottles that's free at every gym in the city. He lands a few good licks, but nothing I can't take. He don't want to dance, though. Keeps coming at me like he's got somewhere else to be tonight. Well, baby, this bout is set for ten rounds. Don't know about you, but I plan on stickin' around awhile.

"What you waiting for?" Swope, my trainer, badgers me in my corner. He's a big man, over six and half feet, with big oven mitts for hands. Used to be in the ring himself, but took a shot to his left eye that damaged a cornea. Now, that eye goes wherever it wants to, seeking out pussy the rest of him can't ever have.

I spit out my mouthpiece. Water from a sponge streams down my face. Feels good to breathe heavy, feel my muscles all pumped up. Iris, she tells me I'm beautiful when I'm in the ring. That's a word I don't hear when people talk about me. Sometimes, when I look in her green eyes, I actually believe it. Baby, I can't wait to go a couple of rounds with you after this is over.

Swope splashes water on my face. "You listening to me? Focus. Don't let him get inside on you."

I spit to my left. Does Swope think I'm a chump? We've been over this a hundred times.

"He'll wear you down on the body if you let him," he says. "Keep him at a distance. Don't waste your punches. Land some points."

I grunt. I don't like to talk much in the ring. Don't talk much outside of it, neither.

Ding!

Round three is mine. I'm feelin' it now. I'm dancin' on air. My punches are lightning bolts. Robbins comes at me, but I stop his charge with a solid right to the cheek. His grunt means it hurt. He shakes it off, comes at me again. I stagger him with another right. He chases me around the ring. My jabs keep him from gettin' to me.

Ding!

Where did the time go? Man, I want more of that stuff.

"Where's Iris?" I ask Swope back in my corner.

"Don't worry about her."

"You ain't seen her yet?"

Swope slaps me on the face. Wakes me up a hell of a lot more than any of Robbins' punches. "Keep your mind in the ring, damn it."

While he sponges me down, I lean my head back and search the front rows for her. I find an empty seat, the only one in sight. Where is she? I'm here for her, but she ain't here for me.

Iris ain't mine. Not yet. She used to be married to Kid Sable. Remember him? The Great White Hope that thought he couldn't lose? He's the one that died a couple of years ago in the ring. Got pummeled the first few rounds, rallied in the fifth and sixth, went down once in the seventh. By the middle of the eighth, both the referee and his trainer threatened to stop the fight. The Kid wouldn't let them. The judge wasn't about to stop it; he was gettin' paid enough grease money to fill both them pockets of his.

The Kid came out for the ninth looking woozy. I remember it like it was yesterday. I stood him up with a couple of jabs before tearing down his body in the middle minute. We clinched in the final seconds. Felt like I was holding us both up. Some champ. That chump couldn't even talk back when I whispered in his ear: "It's gonna feel good inside Iris tonight."

I remember staring at him in his corner before the final round. Arms and legs all splayed out. You can see defeat in a fighter before he'll ever admit it. His head lolled about looking for his girl in the stands. But Iris wasn't there. She told me she didn't want to see it done. All I had to do was take down The Kid. And I did, alright. Took him all the way down.

Ding!

"Get into the game," Swope yells as he pulls the stool out from under me.

Swope is right; Robbins is my opponent tonight, not the Kid. We approach each other warily. By now, each one of us has got the other's moves pretty much figured out. Neither of us wants to do anything stupid. You let your guard down for a second in the ring, next thing you're looking up at a bunch of faces with smelling salts shoved under your nose. I knew one guy who got hit so hard he ended up on the canvas and only remembers the referee counting to "eight". Woke up in the locker room two hours later and sat bolt upright and said, "nine."

A left hook I don't catch jars me. Backed against the ropes. He works my body. I close up. He's trying to get inside, but I slip out. I unleash a flurry that surprises him, but the bell prevents me from doing any real damage. I'm hearing more boos than cheers from the crowd.

"What the hell you doing?" Swope shouts when I'm back in my corner. "You the champ; he ain't nothin'. Don't let him think he ain't. Take it to him before you run out of juice."

"I don't see Iris." I'm trying to look around him, but his body is wide and he positions himself so I can't see past.

"Damn it, "says Swope, "you losin' it."

"Ain't losin' it. Ain't losin' nothing."

Me and Iris. I've had a lot of babes hanging off of me since I started winning fights. Some guys, they don't need to look past a woman's ass or maybe her tits to find what they want. That kinda love is like Chinese food– it's as good hot as it is cold, but you eventually get tired of it just the same unless you sample a new dish. With Iris, it's like steak every night. Juicy and satisfying. You know, I didn't even mind it when she started managing my money and making big decisions for me. Normally, I'd've smacked a girl for pulling that. But not her…that plan she came up with sure sounded as sweet as anything I'd ever thunk up.

"Fight Robbins, damn it." Swope is at me again. "Get that dame out of your head. Before he knocks both of you out."

Ding!

Round five starts off badly for me. Robbins catches me off guard and nails me with a jab-hook-jab combination. Gets me into a corner and starts wailin' on my ribs. I cover up. I land a couple of deflective shots, but take worse than I give. Getting my groove in this round is tough, so I let him chase me around. Pisses off the crowd, me runnin' around like a damn pansy.

When the bell finally sounds, I'm back in my corner laughing at those damn hypocrites in the stands. People pay big bucks to watch us beat each other to a pulp in the ring. They scream for blood, and when they finally get it, they all cover their mouths and shake their heads at what a barbaric sport this is. Like when The Kid died. The Boxing Commission had to open an investigation to satisfy the press. They even waited a month before officially naming me the new champ. Took about eight months before Iris figured the heat had died down enough for us to be seen together in public.

Ding!

I rally in the sixth. Get some good jabs in, score some points. Start showing him why I'm the champ and he's just some young punk. A pretty boy with some hype and a lot of three-piece-suit money behind him. Money that's gonna be filling my pockets thanks to Iris' plan. We got a big chunk riding on this fight. On me. It's all in her name, because I can't bet on my own fights without the Commission suspending me. See, no one knows we've been shacking up together. No one has a clue. No one.

Ding!

I'm in the zone. Can't hear the crowd but I can feel'em. Adrenaline is pumping through me. I bite down hard on my mouthpiece. There's nothing but power in my fists. Before I know it, I'm back in my corner.

"Build on that," Swope tells me.

Why ain't Iris here yet? I stare straight ahead. Even forget to take out my mouthpiece. I think about the last four months leading up to this fight. She got a taste of money after the Kid's death. When she saw the kind of purse a championship fight rakes in, she started with the big ideas. You can bet all kinds of things on boxing besides who wins or loses. Like how long the fight will go or what round someone will score a knockdown. I gotta make the fight go the distance. After I win, we're supposed to go to Tahiti for a month. Maybe get married there.

Ding!

Iris still ain't out there as I move to the center of the ring for round seven. Where the hell is…? Next thing I see is white canvas. I push myself off the ground before the count gets to three. The ref backs me up to a neutral corner. Checks my eyes, my reflexes. Gives me a standing eight count.

"I'm good," I say, bouncing on my feet and shaking it off. "I'm good."

We go back at it. Robbins lands a punch. Another. Another. I feel a sharp pain over my left eye. All night he's been aiming for that spot. I got cut there a week before the bout. Me and Iris were foolin' around and she caught me one by accident. When Swope saw it he hit the roof. Nearly canceled the fight. I couldn't let that happen, what with all of our plans.

Another combination gets through my defenses. I cover up, so he punishes my body. No time to throw a counter. Can't seem to catch my breath.

Ding!

"Call Iris." I'm on my stool and breathing real heavy with my back against the ropes to hold me up. "Where she at?"

"I'm gonna need to call a doctor if you don't get your act together," Swope says. "How'd he find out about that eye?"

I don't answer. Only me, Iris, the doc that patched me up, and Swope know about the weak spot over my eye. I suck in as much air as I can get. Water. Need more water.

Swope massages my neck. "C'mon, now. Show me something."

The ref is standing behind Swope, his hands on his hips. "We still got a fight?"

Swope don't turn around, just looks into my eyes.

I nod once. The ref walks away.

Ding!

Robbins is on fire in round eight. A flurry of jabs, hooks, and uppercuts. He's taggin' me. Won't let up. The ref pulls us apart, warns me about grabbing hold. My muscles are starting to feel heavy. My feet are lead on the canvas. He catches the eye again. The blood makes it impossible to see.

Ding!

I walk back slowly to my corner. Swope crouches down in front of me, puts an *enswell*—a piece of metal dipped in a bucket of cold water—over the bridge of my eye where I'm cut. Puts Vaseline on after. When he looks at me, his face is concerned. Not confident, like the earlier rounds.

"I'm gonna stop it," he says.

"No."

"You don't look good out there."

"No."

He grimaces and shakes his head back and forth slowly, pointing a finger at my face like my old man used to do. "You get smart. Two rounds to go and you're way behind."

Ding!

82

The crowd is going wild. The lights bother my eyes. The sweat and blood make it hard to keep from blinking. Round nine feels like thirty minutes. Gotta stay on my feet. Gotta stay focused. Gotta…

I'm down. The ref counts to five in a watery voice.

Ding!

Swope helps me to my corner.

The ref comes over, but I wave him off. He takes a long look at me. I muster enough energy to raise my gloves in a 'bring it on' motion. He shakes his head back and forth before turning his back as he walks to the center of the ring.

"How many hands I got up?" Swope asks once the ref is gone.

"Three."

Swope looks at his hand to check. "I got one hand up. Three fingers. I'm stopping it."

"Don't."

"It's on you."

Even hurts to nod. "On me."

I think about the Kid and how he looked when he answered the bell for the final round. How he wasn't about to go down. His knees were locked even though his legs were so rubbery a blast of air conditioning could have knocked him over. His eyes were glassy. His mouth hung open. I just kept hitting him. Every clinch I'd hold him up and whisper something about Iris and me. The Kid would try to hit me, but he had nothin' left. He got it before he went down. He knew where his wife had been all those nights he trained and she stayed out late. I saw it in his face just before I put everything into a right cross that collapsed him.

I remember the place got real quiet. The ref didn't even start counting him out. There was a doctor in the ring, his trainer, everyone hovering over him. I could see his white boxing sneakers twitching on the canvas. They took him out on a stretcher. The Kid went into a coma and died at the hospital four days later.

Ding!

I pull myself up for the final round. Everything looks jerky. I feel like a punching bag. Can hardly catch my breath or keep on my feet. Don't want to move. Just holding onto Robbins. "Iris," he whispers in my ear as the ref pries us apart. Jab. Uppercut. Uppercut. Hook. They just keep coming. As I fall into a clinch with him, I'm feelin' nauseous. I can taste his sweat. His breath is in my ear.

"She wants to be with the best," Robbins says as he lands a couple of body shots.

I struggle against him. We split. He lands a couple grazing shots and then we're back in another clinch.

83

"She had an eye for you, and one for me," he says.

Robbins pushes me away and lands another on my weak left eye. It's completely closed. I don't know where my hands are. My legs are drained. There's a ringing in my ears. Time is stuck. A tidal wave hits me and I surf through the air. When I land on the shore, I bounce back up again so the ref won't even think about stopping the fight.

See, I know she started seeing Robbins while I trained. A bird only learns one way to fly. Before my standing eight count is over, I look over at her sitting ringside. I give her a smirk. Her eyes narrow and her mouth gets all scrunched up. Kind of reminds me of the Kid when he figured it all out. By then, it was too late for him, too.

But, that's not how this story is going to end. I come out of the eight count a man possessed. Robbins spends the next two minutes learning how to bleed and hurt all over again. My fists are pistons that can't stop pounding. He goes down once. Twice. I can see the glassy look in his eyes. He's probably got two of me in his sights and don't know which one to hit—the chump he thought I was or the man that's about to finish him off.

I'm relentless as time winds down on us both. If he stays on his feet, he wins the fight. I gotta lay him out. His head is bobbing around and I know that to him I look like one of them funhouse mirrors where your body is all out of focus and stretched out. The last punch is for both him and Iris. He falls hard, like I did for her, but his fall is one he won't get up from. He lies on the canvas like one of them crash-test dummies. It's bright as all hell in the ring, but darkness is probably closing in on him like when the lights come down before the film starts. This is my movie, Jack. And you ain't got a part in it no more.

And Iris, she's just staring ahead, probably wondering what happened to that very same movie Robbins was waitin' on. But, there's nothing on the screen, and she can't figure it out. Maybe the projector is broken.

For a brief moment I lock eyes with her. I wonder if it's all clear to her now. I wonder if she realizes she's lost.

They raise my arm up high. I'm still the champ. Swope is gabbing about how he knew I had it in me. There's a ringing in my ears. It's rattlin' through my head. Robbins knocked me around pretty good. Not nearly as much as Iris is gonna get. The bookie she placed the bet with? Old pal of mine. He's getting a cut of the money that is all going to me. No way she'll tell the cops or anyone after I take that money from her. All I gotta do is remind her what she did to her husband, the Kid. Because I'm the only one who knows about the bruised rib she gave him the night before the fight. The one I worked on until it finally broke and punctured his lung.

I'm the champ, both in the ring and out.

Legwork

I lost the use of my legs when I was seventeen. Breaking and entering came a lot easier than geometry and physics, so while my peers were cutting class to smoke behind school, I was busting into their homes. While trying to get away from some pissed Italian lady whose place I'd just hit, I ended up on the roof. My attempt to jump to freedom fell a couple of bloody fingernails short. My life passed me by in three short stories. I landed in a poor excuse for a garden between two non-descript tenements of New York City. Broke my back and shattered both my legs.

Being a cripple can work to your advantage. Since I couldn't run with the pack, I adapted to my wheelchair the best I could. I spent a lot of time alone, making my hands agile instead of idle. Breaking and entering was out, so I hustled tourists downtown with sleight of hand cons and card tricks. I got so smooth the Manhattan streets came to know me as 'Nimble' Kimble. People heaped money and apologies on the helpless cripple. Never respect or admiration. Those were two things I could never swindle.

Cripples can't be crooks, right? Put on a nice, respectable suit, and I could sell contact lenses to a blind man. Being the object of pity became the best career move I ever made. No one suspects a disabled person of casing banks and jewelry stores. As for being ID'ed? Everyone remembers a guy in a wheelchair, but no one ever looks in your eyes. Most people can't even recall my hair color. And what could be more convenient for a getaway car than handicapped parking right in front of the joint?

I hooked up with Marco's bunch six years ago. With my unique talents I figured bigger money lay in teaming up. We moved jewelry, rare coins, cell phones. Anything that sold easily. Marco grew up in Hell's Kitchen, so he knew all the wrong people in all the most fucked-up places. He latched onto New York crime like a newborn sucking a tit, draining as much life out of the streets as he could.

Spezio grew up with Marco. His head was so far up the boss' ass he could see through his eyes. He looked like Eminem without the stupid clothes; a white boy who hated blacks but wished he could be dope like them. Which was funny because our triggerman, Harris, was a darkie with the personality of a crowbar. I heard he was a linebacker in college who took a few hits too many to the helmet. He was virtually a mute. His fists did most of his talking. I once saw him hit a guy so hard that three of the dude's teeth flew out of his mouth.

My share was less than everyone else's. Every time I'd complain they come back with the same old lines.

"All you do is drive," said Marco.

"Yeah," Spezio chimed in. "You don't do any legwork." He let out a snigger, belatedly figuring out his own pun.

"What about Harris?" I asked. "I been around longer than he has."

"Him being a nigger gets him less," said Marco. "Him being a badass nigger makes you even. Him being a badass nigger with a gun entitles him to a bigger cut."

"Yeah," said Spezio. "Just be glad you ain't a nigger."

Harris' eyes roved back and forth during the conversation, those pupils speaking volumes, black ink on blood-red pages.

"One of these days I'm gonna bust out on my own," I said. "What do I got to lose?"

"There's always something else to lose," said Marco.

*   *   *

The miracle happened nine weeks ago out in the Hamptons. A single cop car pursued the mini-van I was driving. I always stole automatics, so I could use a little club I rigged up for accelerating in lieu of my dormant legs. Steer with the left hand and gas it with the right. The school bus emerged in front of me before I could react. The impact was enough to send those kids back a few grades. The bus skidded down the lane and keeled over like a dazed fighter. My mini-van slammed into the sidewalk nose first and rolled a couple of times to make sure it stayed down for the count. As I lay amongst the stink of gasoline and burning rubber, I heard the high-pitched screams of kids mingled with the music from the still-working van radio. A cop car screeched to a stop on the other side of my defeated mini-van came as I crawled from the wreckage. His receding footsteps were a break for me; he opted to check the kids first.

I wasn't going to get very far on torn up hands without my chair. That's when I noticed a peculiar sensation. I looked down at my right foot. My shoe was gone, the sock singed away to the heel. My foot bled, warm red liquid dripping between my toes. It tickled.

My left leg ached like it weighed a couple hundred pounds I couldn't move. After all of those years of muscle atrophy any type of feeling down there both enthralled and scared me. After the initial shock, I began pulling my torso away from the wreck. The van had landed in a park near some bushes, so I headed for the cover they afforded. When I got there, I lifted myself up a light pole. My feet refused to support the weight of my body. I slid back to the ground and crawled onward.

Some picnickers had left a blanket on the grass. The commotion must have emptied the immediate area of the park as concerned citizens ran to pull future lawyers and policemen out of the overturned school bus. I stole the blanket and continued to crawl towards a park bench twenty yards away. My lower limbs began to tingle. The feeling of pain from the cuts was exhilarating. Before trashing my soiled gray shirt I used it wipe away the blood. Aside from sweat, my black t-shirt underneath was relatively clean. I sat with the stolen blanket over my awakening legs and waited. If you didn't know me, I looked almost normal.

I had a sketchy moment when two patrolmen canvassing the area stopped to ask if I saw anyone running through the park. I told them I heard the crash, but being a paraplegic was unable to assist when I saw people running across the field. They looked down at the blanket covering my withered legs. I revealed one of my atrophied twigs from under the blanket as proof, and damned if they didn't believe me. No, I didn't see anyone go this way. Sure, here's my address and telephone number, neither of which were correct.

Luckily I still had my phone to reach Marco. I told him about the accident, but nothing else. No one needed to know about something shifting in my spine so that my legs might work again. He sent Spezio to come get me.

"You gonna need a new wheelchair," Spezio said as we drove away from the park.

"Yeah," I said. "I'm gonna need a lot of new things."

* * *

The next few weeks I spent building up the strength in my forgotten limbs. Before long I was walking. I'd slip out at night and roam the streets. In recent years I didn't even dream about using my legs again, and here I was running down dark alleys showing off to the shadows. I started busting into places at night, just for the fun of it.

I still used the wheelchair during the day. The temptation to display my sudden mobility was overwhelming, but I bided my time. Crooks are creatures of habit. If things are going right, you don't do anything to tempt fate. That's how you get caught. There were days I wanted to jump out of the chair and kick Spezio in the ass or run to the store for a case of beer to prove I was worth more to Marco than he figured. But I had a better, more lucrative idea. My legs could carry me out of the rut my life was stuck in. When the time was right I would rip off my own crew. And no matter what town I fled to, Marco would go looking for a cripple.

*　*　*

It was a gray November day when I drove a stolen silver Lexus by the Fine Art of Jewelry. I pulled about fifty feet past the store and dropped off Marco, Spezio and Harris. As soon as they were out of the car, I put aside my accelerator stick and used my feet to work the pedals, the motions now second nature after my nocturnal practice of the past two months.

The alley where I kept the Lexus purring afforded me a good view of the jewelry store across the street. Waiting was brutal. Sometimes I could swear the hands on my watch moved backward. Finally, the agreed upon time arrived. I was out in the street, tires screeching and heading for the door just as Spezio burst out the front and fell to the ground. He rolled over and writhed on his side. His blood stained the sidewalk.

Then the earthquake hit. At least, that's what it felt like. I never saw the green SUV leap out of the opposite alley. A loud crunch married the two vehicles. My door flew open and the impact nearly threw me out of the car. The seatbelt saved me from being a red Rorschach blotch on the pavement.

I guess the smart thing would have been to get the hell out of there. But the smart thing is something hindsight sticks in your face because you can't change the past. Harris and Marco were still inside. I scrambled out of the car, ignoring the protests of the suited guy from the van waving his arms, registration in one hand and insurance card in the other. Cops would be around within minutes, so I had to be quick. My day had come at last.

I stepped over Spezio and gave his inert body a hard kick. Red ooze flowed out of the side of his neck. I flanked the doorway and listened to the shouting inside.

"Damn it, Harris." Marco shouted. "What the hell are you doing?"

"You were going to leave me and take the stuff, you piece of shit." It was probably the first full sentence I ever heard out of Harris.

I could see inside enough to locate Harris on the floor hording a black bag. He was leaning on his left elbow, a gun in his hand. His right hand was buried under his stomach, probably where he got shot.

"Dude, we got about two minutes to get out of here," Marco said.

Harris sucked hard for air. "You son of a bitch…"

I dove into the room, rolled, and ended up on my feet looking down on Harris. Marco was about fifteen feet away, leaning on the counter that ran along the far wall. I could see the motionless torso of a guy—probably the shop owner—lying behind the right counter. Broken glass from the far display tore into the chest and arm of another body to Marco's left.

Harris and Marco gaped at me.

"How the fuck...?" Harris didn't finish his sentence. I stepped down on his wrist and kicked the gun from his hand. It skidded a few feet away from him. I picked it up and shot him straight between his eyes. The force of the bullet cleared him off the bag of jewels. Keeping a bead on Marco, I bent over and picked up the bounty.

"Nimble," said Marco, "you son of a bitch. You been stringing us along for all these years?"

"Naw," I said as I raised the gun. "You always had a leg up on me. Two, in fact."

The first bullet went through his protesting palm. He looked with disbelief at the bloody hole in his right hand. "Listen, buddy." His tone was desperate. "Split fifty-fifty, you don't have to..."

I finished the sentence for him with an exclamation mark as the second bullet ripped into his neck and toppled him to the ground in a heap.

It was perfect. I'd take the loot; they'd take the fall. I always wore gloves when I drove, so fingerprints were not a concern. I dropped the gun near Harris and figured I'd let the cops fend for themselves on who killed who. The black bag was heavy but I shoved it inside my jacket as I stepped over the body behind the counter. The back door and sweet freedom lay straight ahead. I was reaching for the knob when I heard the shot.

A shock rang through my body. The bag of jewels slipped from my grip as I fell against the wall. Everything got hot and fuzzy. My cheek scraped down the wall. The floor tasted like blood. I had just enough energy left to roll over and see the shop owner's gun arm fall to the ground next to his body. As I passed out, I couldn't help but laugh.

* * *

I blinked my eyes and looked around the hospital room. Lots of white, a color I wasn't used to in living situations. Bars covered a window that allowed precious little sunlight in. A fly buzzed around the sheets at my feet. I wanted to kick it away. Nothing happened. I tried again. My legs lay there as inert as they'd been since I was seventeen. To my left was an intravenous drip. Probably Demerol or Morphine from the way my head floated. Maybe this whole deal about getting my legs back was just a dream, a drug-induced trip through my imagination. Was this where I ended up after hitting that school bus two months ago?

The fly landed on my cheek. I tried to swat him away with my hand. Nothing. The fly remained on my face. I tried again to raise my arm to smack him. The little beast moved his stick figure legs like a boxer going through quick combinations, taunting me to counter. I began to sweat, unable to move either arm to bat him away. There was no response or feeling in any of my limbs. My arms had become as useless as my legs.

The fly walked around my face, each movement on my skin an insult. The little monster finally flew away to avoid the tear rolling down from my eye.

I guess Marco was right. There always is something more to lose.

Life Saver

The drive to Nederland takes a good twenty minutes up the winding mountain roads in good weather. I was cruising up Canyon Road as hail pelted white marbles on my windshield. Heavy winds made it tough to keep the car between the lines. Country music battled with static on my radio as I climbed further away from civilization. Evening had just fallen and the headlights slicing through the dark made the street glisten.

The only reason I saw her was the brief glint from her flashlight. My first opportunity to pull over was a hundred yards up the road at a scenic stop around the bend. A minute later I saw her loping towards the car, a huddled bundle bathed in red as she passed by my taillights. When she came abreast to the passenger door, I switched off the radio and threw the auto-lock. The door opened and she plopped down on the seat in a soggy heap with a knapsack on her lap.

She sneezed and rubbed her hands for warmth. "You're a life saver." Water dripped from her face and long hair onto the gearshift.

"You sure picked a bad night to break down," I said.

"When is there a good night for it?"

"Suppose you're right." I shifted into gear and fed the car some gas to continue the climb to Nederland. Visibility was almost non-existent.

She shifted in her seat as we veered back onto the road. Mud covered her shoes all the way up to the knees of her jeans. Even with her face battered by the elements, I could see she was pretty in a rugged sort of way. The kind you hoped would fill in the lines with color once you heard what she had to say. She was young enough to be my daughter, probably just out of college. The sound of the tires on the caution bumps separating the lanes brought my attention back to the road.

"What's your name?" I asked.

"Valerie," she said staring ahead. "What's yours?"

"Brett Singo." I noticed a slight stiffening in her posture. She turned and gave me a brief smile as she reached into the front pocket of her knapsack and pulled out some tissues. When she blew her nose, the motion caused a long flashlight to slip out of her bag. A red stain glistened on the shaft. She used her free hand to shove it back inside the knapsack.

"I didn't see your car," I said. "But, then again, I wasn't looking for it either."

A kind of laugh slipped out, a little hysterical, like when the joke is private. "I went off the road."

"You must have been *way* off the road."

The sound of a safety clicking off is like no other. When she pulled her hand out of the knapsack pocket, the gun was in clear view and pointing at my midsection. "You talk too much."

A sheet of rain slapped the window. "What happened back there, Valerie?"

Hearing her name made her flinch. "I didn't do anything."

"You're doing something now, and it ain't good."

The gun wavered in her hands. I started to pull off the road at another scenic stop.

"No! Keep driving."

I veered back onto the road. "Where to?"

"Nederland. We were supposed to go there."

"We?"

She breathed in short bursts and wiped tears and snot away from her nose. "Just shut up and drive."

I gave the car some more gas. We were traveling a good twenty miles over the speed limit, a dangerous speed on these windy roads even in good weather. The headlights caressed the occasional guardrails on the sloped side of the road. Her teeth started to chatter to I cranked up the heater.

"He's dead," she said without any provocation.

"Who's dead?"

"Billy." A wave of anguish racked her body. Her gun arm sagged. I was more afraid of her shooting me by accident than anything else.

"Who's Billy?"

"Billy Dobbs."

"Did you kill him?"

"No!" Her gun arm straightened as if *I* had killed Billy. "I heard the shot. I saw him put Billy in the car and push it down the ravine."

"Maybe he's not dead. Maybe he's..."

Her crying intensified. "I saw him," she sobbed. "His face. His beautiful face was smashed into the windshield. There was so much blood..." Her gun arm sagged from a weight heavier than the six or so pounds of metal. "We were supposed to go skiing this weekend."

The hail had ceased but rain still sprinkled down. A crash of thunder hinted we weren't out of the storm yet.

"He's dead." She said it with a lack of finality, like she hoped I could somehow contradict her. Her head dipped to her chest. I made the mistake of laying a comforting hand on her shoulder. The gun resumed its position pointing at my stomach.

"Don't touch me."

"Sorry." I slowly took my hand off of her shoulder. "I'm just trying to help you."

"How can you possibly help me?"

"If you didn't kill Billy, then who did?"

"Just drive," she said.

A few miles later we passed the Nederland city line. Which meant that every so often we could see lights on in houses way up the hill. In the distance was the main city, which added up to a handful of streets with a smattering of businesses. It was a one-horse town that had been put out to pasture long ago.

"Turn left here."

We turned onto a paved road that soon became gravel. Each time we turned the road got smaller and bumpier. When the headlights revealed a dead end with nothing but trees past it, I put the cark in park and left the engine idling. We sat in silence for a good minute. Her voice cracked when she spoke.

"No one will believe me."

"Try me," I said.

"Why should I tell you anything?"

"Look, I pulled over to help because you were stranded on a country road in the middle of nowhere in a hailstorm. You pull a gun and hijack me up into the backwoods to go I don't know where. The way I see it, what have either of us got to lose at this point?

She laughed at that. "You sound like a cop. I've got a record, you know."

"Who doesn't these days?" I turned in the seat to face her. "What kind of record?"

She looked away, the gun going slack again. Her arm had to be getting tired by now. "Possession. Two times. If I get nabbed again, I'm done."

"Was Billy buying or selling?"

"Selling," she said.

I nodded once, though she probably didn't notice. "Put the gun down."

"No."

"Okay, don't put the gun down." I turned the car off. The rain made plopping sounds all around the car. "What now?"

She thought about it for a good thirty seconds. "Give me the car keys."

"Why should I..."

"Give me the car keys or so help me God I'll shoot you."

When someone spells out what they're going to do like that, it's a sure bet if they haven't already done it, they never will. I was feeling more confident about the gun, even though it was still pointing at me. I gave her the keys, knowing full well that she'd make a mistake sooner rather than later.

We both stepped out of the car into the cold darkness. There were no streetlights and the clouds held the moon hostage. I smelled dung. The rain, which would soon turn to sleet or snow, made a wall of white noise that masked the normal sounds of the wilderness. She took her flashlight out of the knapsack and flicked it on.

"Take this," she said.

I didn't want to get my fingerprints on a potential murder weapon. My gloves were in my pocket, so I got those out slowly so as not to spook her. "Pretty cold out here." Once the gloves were on, I took the flashlight. It was one of those heavy, silver Mag-lites, the kind that could double as a nightstick. The blood on the handle was still sticky.

"Did someone hit Billy with this?"

"No, I used it to..." Choked sobs stifled the rest of the sentence. She nudged me in the back with the gun. "See that opening in the trees over there?"

I raised the flashlight and searched in the vicinity where she pointed until I located the path. "Yeah."

"You walk and I'll follow. If that flashlight goes out, I'm going to shoot you and take your car."

"Sounds like a plan."

We walked into the darkened woods. Our feet sluicing in the mud and the rain slapping the earth were the only sounds I heard until she started talking. It sounded more like confessor to priest than gunman to hostage.

"Me and Billy, well, Billy was dealing. Mostly coke, but this time we, uh...he decided to try heroin. It's pretty big with the college kids around here and up in Nederland. With coke, we do the drop right in Boulder along the walking mall. No one pays attention. But the heroin guy, he wanted to do the exchange at one of the stops on the road to Nederland.

"Billy had me hang out behind a rock cropping. He didn't want the guy to see me. I saw this big guy in one of those outback ranger jackets with the big flaps. He and Billy talked for a couple of minutes. They weren't arguing or anything. Next thing I know there's a gunshot and I see Billy fall to the ground. The guy in the coat is looking down on him, pointing the gun at his face. When he hit Billy with the gun..."

94

Something rustled in the bushes. She sucked in her breath and then let it out slowly. It was probably just a rabbit or a squirrel.

"Billy stopped moving. The guy dragged him into our car and stuck him in the front seat." A tremble came into her voice. "He started pushing the car towards the ravine...I tried to get to him before the car went over the edge...it was raining so hard...then the car went over..." She was hyperventilating and trying not to cry. "I hit him. I hit him with the flashlight."

"Who did you hit?"

It took her a few breaths to calm down.

"He fell down the hill after the car, but not all the way. He wasn't moving. At my feet was this gun. I guess I picked it up. I heard another shot and felt something like a bumblebee whiz past my head. I ran into the woods further down the road and hid until I heard his car drive away. You came along about ten minutes later."

"So you clocked the guy who killed Billy and took his gun, but he still got away. And he's armed."

"I wish I killed him." Her voice held the kind of violence reserved for afterthoughts.

"Where are we going now?" I asked.

"Shut up." Her voice had become defiant now that she'd exorcised her guilt.

I tripped a couple times on roots buried in the muddy path. My clothes were totally drenched. After a hard turn around a cropping of rocks, I saw the outline of a cabin snuggled amidst the trees. I walked up the creaky steps to a porch that felt like it would barely hold my weight. We stood there waiting for something to happen, the sound of our collective breathing in the slapping rain the only thing separating us in the darkness.

"You're a cop, aren't you?" she said.

"Yeah."

"Why haven't you arrested me or something?"

"You have the gun, remember?"

"Let's go inside."

I pushed the door open and went inside with her behind me. A switch flicked on and lit up the place. It was a two-room deal. The backroom was probably a bedroom. The front room looked like a redneck fraternity house. A beat-up couch with a bunch of old blankets for upholstery sat unevenly on a threadbare carpet. Two old wooden chairs and a fake leather recliner joined the couch around a piece of wood supported by cinderblocks. A pot bellied stove was in one corner of the room. In the far corner was a small sink and aluminum counter next to a decrepit refrigerator. All the comforts of home...if you were used to trailer living.

I turned to face her. "What do we do now?"

She scanned the room. Her eyes blinked back tears and her lower lip quivered. The damn gun was still clutched in her hand, though it no longer had her attention. The sound of boots against wood jerked her out of whatever daydream or nightmare the cabin conjured in her head. Someone walked up the first step, then the second.

She pointed with the gun. "Over there."

We moved toward the far side of the room so that we could face the front door.

"Should we turn out the lights?" she asked.

"Little late for that."

We waited. The intruder wasn't in any hurry. I heard steps going back and forth along the porch.

"Give me the gun," I whispered.

She looked at me like I was crazy.

"I'm a cop. I can kill him before he kills you or me."

She handed the gun over reluctantly. Her fear of me was less than towards the intruder. My gloved hand slipped around the handle and my finger nestled around to the trigger.

The doorknob turned. The door made a creaking sound as it slowly opened. The person hesitated then walked inside the cabin. He was a large man in a drab olive outback jacket. He had a face ruddy from the cold and his thinning hair was plastered to his head. Some blood had seeped into his collar from a wound to the back of his head.

Valerie pointed with her free hand. "That's him!"

The man stopped and stared at us in disbelief. "Son of a bitch." His startled face grew stern when he focused on the girl. He took a confident step forward.

"Shoot him," she said. "He killed Billy. That bastard killed Billy."

I raised the gun to chest level and pointed it at the intruder. He stopped and jerked back.

"You killed Billy Dobbs over a heroin deal?" I said. I could see the bloody part of his skull near his ear where she had hit him with the flashlight.

He didn't put his hands up in protest. "Listen, all I did—"

I extended the gun further in his direction, which shut him up.

"You're a cop," Valerie shouted, "Shoot him!"

I turned and shot her in the hole her lips made in silent protest. The force of the bullet slammed her body into the corner where it wedged momentarily before sliding to the floor, leaving a bloody smear on the wall.

"Damn, Singo," the man in the outback jacket said. He peeled it off to reveal a deputy's uniform. "When I came in here and saw you and Dobbs' girl, I almost shit myself." He gingerly touched the side of his head and

96

looked at the blood glistening on his hand. "Damn bitch beaned me pretty good."

"You shot Billy Dobbs?" I asked.

"Hell, no, man. I used these." He held up two massive hands that I knew to be lethal weapons. "Billy tried to shoot me after I hit him, but I got the gun out of his hands and knocked him out. Put him in the car and dumped him down the canyon."

"That's not how she tells it."

"She was hiding. How the hell she see *anything* in this rain?"

"What were you doing dealing heroin to him? I don't pay you enough?"

"Hell, man." He dipped his head like a kid with his hand caught in the cookie jar.

"Where's the heroin and Billy's money?"

"In my car."

"This your gun?" I held up the weapon that I used to paint the walls with Valerie's brains.

"His. You wouldn't want me firing one of ours." He patted his side where I knew his service weapon was holstered. The one he probably fired at her after she pushed him into the ravine.

"Guess you can't be too careful."

He relaxed and took a step towards me.

I shot Deputy Vance Stubbs through the heart with Billy Dobbs' gun. Vance looked almost as surprised as Valerie had. He was a huge man, so I shot him again, just to make sure. It's bad enough when a cop turns, and even worse when he crosses one of his own.

Can't have any free agents cutting in on my business.

Snakes in the Grass

I was about to uncover the sarcophagus deep inside a great king's tomb when two hands grabbed me. Awakening in my London flat to my wife Jeanette's hysterical face couldn't have been more alarming if I had really been in that ancient burial site. She had me by the shoulders and shook hard. "Peter, come quickly. It's Brent. Oh, my God. Oh, my God!"

I pushed her away, still trying to get my wits about me. The clock confirmed the time to be a good two hours before my normal seven am wake-up. The air in our bedroom was as cold as an archaeological dig.

"Hurry, goddamn you!" she shrieked. "We've got to do something."

Rolling to my side, I slid my feet to the floor and located my slippers. I stood up and yawned. The place wasn't on fire and England hadn't been subject to bombing for many a decade. "Calm down and tell me what's the matter?"

"We've got to help Brent." She was trembling. I reached to put my arms on her but she swatted them away. "He'll die, he'll die."

My brain finally began to wake with the rest of my body. Brent was our border. "Calm down. Where is he?"

She pointed out the door. "In bed."

I followed her down the hall. At the door to the spare bedroom, she turned and put her hands up.

"We need to go in slowly." Her voice quivered and her eyes were red-rimmed. "So we don't startle it."

"Startle what?"

"The snake," she whispered.

"Snake? Don't be absurd."

The crack in the door beckoned ominously. I moved her aside and pushed on the solid wood, which made a creaking sound accompanied by Jeanette's intake of breath.

Gray light snuck into the room through the sheer beige curtains covering the ground floor window, a dreary London morning reluctantly climbing out of its crypt. Brent lay in bed at a skewed angle, his head slanting uncomfortably away from his naked chest. A crumpled blanket and sheet covered him from the waist down. His eyes, riveted on a hollow in the covers, didn't move when I came in.   Sweat covered him as if he were gripped by a fever.

I took a step into the room.

"Don't," Brent whispered without moving.

"C'mon, Brent." I took another step towards the bed. "What's the ruse?"

"Please." He sounded desperate, almost heroic.

The terror in his eyes made me stop short. "What is it?"

He remained inert. His lips barely parted when he spoke. "A snake. Under the covers."

"It's probably just a garter snake that crept in," I tried to reassure him. His gaunt face told me otherwise. And he was a man who knew a *Thamnophis marcianus* from a *Vipera transcuacasiana*.

"Poisonous," he said. "I think it's a viper."

Jeanette's inhale was cut short by fear. Without taking my eyes off of Brent I calmly directed her. "Go get the poker from the fireplace and the axe by the woodpile."

When I didn't hear any movement behind me, I turned to see her blinking away tears. "Hurry," I whisper-shouted.

Once she was gone, I turned back to survey the situation. Brent's chest rose and fell, his finely chiseled muscles slick with perspiration. Last year when he hit forty, I marveled that it had yet to start hitting back. His rugged face, previously unmarred with the lines and creases of age, seemed to have eroded overnight.

I pointed at a puffy area near his crotch. "Is that where the snake is?" His eyebrows went up and down twice. I wasn't about to ask the pointless question of how it got there.

"Okay," I said. "Stay calm. Jeanette will be back in a flash."

He blinked his acknowledgement.

I looked down upon him so helpless in my guest room bed. Four years ago, he was one of many workers at the 30 Gresham Street dig in London under my supervision. My status as the youngest member in charge of a team garnered both pride and resentment from others. Brent, though older than me, accepted his task of logging what we found. The man would never ascend the ladder of superiority in the archaeological field; the only actual digging he would get to do would be to unearth facts buried in old catalogs.

At Gresham Street I excavated a life-sized left hand and forearm of a gilded, cast bronze statue from 70 AD. Since it was found among vast amounts of broken pottery in an oval-shaped pond that contained waterlogged sediments indicative of standing water, I deduced the arm must

99

have been part of some public statue that had been hacked apart and dumped in the site.

There isn't much money in archaeology. My meager salary bolstered by Jeanette's inheritance and wages as a secretary afforded us a modest flat in Chalk Farm. Although space is tight, we rented Brent a bedroom for pittance at the culmination of the Gresham Street dig. He was good dinner company and his presence made me feel less guilty when I was called away to sites such as Peru to assist in the Chavin de Hunatar dig.

Jeanette tiptoed into the room with the black iron poker in her right hand and the worn metal axe in her left looking like a modern day Joan of Arc. Her beautiful face and generously proportioned figure had always invoked jealousy whenever we were at parties. I never questioned why she chose me for her husband. Or why she chose Brent as her lover in my own home.

I reached behind me. "The poker."

Jeanette placed the handle in my palm. The iron felt cold and dispassionate. I crept to the bed, making as little noise as possible. As I came nearer, the covers moved just about where his knee should be. The snake's smooth scales brushed the sheet audibly. Brent stifled his breathing as he tried to remain completely still. I could detect the outline of the lazily coiled snake under the sheet.

"I'm going to use the poker to slowly lift the sheets by your feet," I said. "That way, if the snake is startled, it'll hopefully take umbrage with the poker and not you."

The sheets were soaked all around him. I swear I could hear his heart thumping in his chest. His eyes begged me. With the utmost care, I maneuvered the poker at the foot of the bed and placed the sharp edge under the sheet and blanket.

"Oh, God, please…" Jeanette prayed.

"He made all creatures," I said as I slowly raised the covers with the poker. "Though some were not meant to lie together." My hand strained under the weight of the metal as I willed my nerves to remain calm. The sheet rose higher and higher like a ghostly spirit awakening. The clump of snake didn't move.

I elevated the sheets a foot off the bed. I could now see the brownish shades of the snake, so incongruous with the white sheets. *Bothrops atrox*, a very deadly pit viper snake better known as the Common Lancehead. Just another inch or so…

The weight of the blanket shifted and slipped from the poker. Though still covered, I could see the snake's head darting in alarm. There was scream. Reflexively, I threw the poker to my right. The snake lashed out in a fluid, yet swift motion. The snap of its deadly fangs sent a chill down my spine. Missing the poker, its head reeled around and recoiled, staring at Brent who was frozen with panic. He didn't dare make a move or the snake would have at him.

Jeanette whined like a little girl. "Brent…"

"Shut up," I said.

The snake's broad, triangular head turned, taking us in for the first time. It hissed its disapproval, the black tongue slipping in and out between the lethal fangs. Deeming us unworthy of attention after a few breath-stopping moments, it turned its interest back to Brent. The pit viper slithered in circular arcs as it repositioned itself in the furrows of the sheets.

Brent squeezed his eyes shut. Though muscular, his full nakedness next to the snake's grandeur rendered him the weaker species. Jeanette sobbed quietly behind me.

For just a moment I marveled at the deadly viper. Its thick body coiled like a precision machine. The snake looked to be nearly four feet long, if stretched to full length. Brown and white markings geometrically adorned its body in descending patterns. Heavily keeled scales covered its lithe form, a single muscle working in perfect harmony. The lancehead kept its dead bronze eyes on Brent, almost daring him to make a move.

"I'm going to distract it," I said, looking at Brent. "When I do, you get the hell out of there."

Jeanette put her hands on my shoulders and buried her head into my back. Sharp fingernails dug into my skin. "No, no, no."

She hadn't touched me so passionately in months. The feel of her hands on my body reminded me of why I needed her, and why I couldn't allow myself to be swayed by her perfection. Sometimes beauty is best seen from afar so familiarity cannot tarnish it. Like the buried treasures of Tutankhamen in Luxor, their exquisiteness is best seen in a museum when they are nice and cleaned up rather than buried in centuries-old dirt. The more I excavated my wife's personality, the more I realized she was fool's gold.

I straightened up and arched my shoulders away from her grasp. "Give me the axe."

When I turned, I saw her staring down at the floor where it lay. Grimacing at her uselessness, I bent over and picked it up. I stood up and put my free hand behind her neck and ran my fingers through her disheveled hair.

"Calm down," I said into her ear. I could smell the intoxicating sweetness of her skin going sour. "I'm going to need your help on this."

A sickly sound escaped from her throat.

I stroked her mane of hair with an assuring, "Shhhhh…I'm going to smash that bastard to hell. What I need you to do is stick close to him."

Still shaking, her head told me 'no.'

"Do you want him to live?" I asked.

The tears escaped from her eyes before her legs gave out. I had to struggle to keep her from hitting the floor with my one free arm. After I hefted her back up, our eyes met. I saw into her heart and for one moment I felt empathy. The moment soon passed.

"Jeanette," I said. "You can do this. For Brent."

She took an unsteady, but deep breath. "For Brent."

I positioned her by the bed close to his chest. The back of her damp nightgown felt clammy against my steadying hand. Placing myself towards the back of the viper, I knew I had one chance to get this right. One bite from the snake would be sure death, no matter how quickly the victim reached the hospital. The venom yield of the *Bothrops atrox* averages 124 milligrams per bite, twice the lethal 62 milligrams dose.

Brent and me locked eyes. "As archaeologists," I said to him, "the only thing we can't dig up is love." I raised my right arm with the blunt side of the axe towards the bed. His eyes grew wide with realization and fear. "But, we can bury it."

In one fluid motion I shoved Jeanette down onto the bed and smashed the butt end of the axe onto the crown of Brent's head. The dull crack from his skull was nearly drowned by the screams from my wife's flailing body as the startled snake struck again and again.

I pounded his skull once more. His flesh and bone relented with a sickening squishing noise. My other hand kept Jeanette smothered onto the snake. I released and jumped back quickly to watch the lovers do a final spastic dance together, far enough away to prevent any reprisal from the agitated viper.

Rivulets of blood flowed down the sides of Brent's head like lava oozing out of a volcano. Jeanette slid to the floor, probably in shock from the venom coursing through her veins. She'd be joining Brent in a matter of minutes as the hemotoxin paralyzed and eventually killed her. The snake writhed on the bed, biting Brent's leg once for good measure.

I ran to the closet and grabbed mace to debilitate the viper. A few sprays made it impotent. Flipping the axe over, I hacked the viper into little pieces to be buried along with the two bodies. A pang of sadness racked my body as I sunk to my knees. Three lives had ended, not just two. I closed my eyes as a requiem for myself as well as the two lovers. Did any one of us get what we deserved? I'd venture to respond in negative. But, love is like that sometimes.

Someday, thousands of years from now, archaeologists may uncover the remains of two specimens of our day and age. I doubt they'd ever be able to piece together the story of those lives based on the causes of death.

The history of our lineage is not written by how we died, but by how we lived. I will continue to search for the answers to the past as I don't see much hope for our species in the future.

Death Insurance

The sign on the door read Reginald Dennis, Death Insurance Adjusting and Sales. A slogan below the official title stated 'Don't Let Life Get You Up–2300 Years of Permanence' in robust, cursive lettering. He pushed open the door and walked in.

Dennis, dressed in a powder blue suit, sat behind a simple mahogany desk polished to a handsome shine revealing striations in the wood's natural beauty. The top was devoid of any files, pencils, or other regular accouterments. The window behind him was as white as the endless walls that made up the 'office.'

"I'm Reginald Dennis." He stood up and offered a hand, smiling wider than necessary. With neat sandy hair above a freckled face he looked too young to be able to ensure that anyone would remain dead. "Please sit down."

A chair materialized at the desk facing the insurance adjuster.

"How may I be of service?" Exuberance emanated from the man. "And, please call me Reg. If we're talking about death and life matters, we should be on a first name basis."

"Thank you…Reg." He sat down with a swish of his dirty white robe.

"Ah, I can see you're a little unsure." 'Reg' sat back in a reclining position to take in his client. Although the customer's hair was scraggly and unkempt, a neatly trimmed beard of fine brown hair covered a weak chin. Two eyes that could only be characterized as 'searching' held court over a streamlined nose, thin lips, and skin that had seen a lot of hardship. "This type of coverage can be a little overwhelming at first. Perhaps you're here to ask about our discounted death insurance?"

"Your company claims that I will never return among the living. You've got quite a reputation"

Reg sloughed off the compliment, but was obviously pleased. "We've worked hard to attain such status. Allow me to inquire if you're interested in basic death insurance or one of our term policies?"

"Term policies?" The client leaned back with a swish of his dirty white robe.

"Yes, they've become quite popular these days. We first came out with them around 450 A.D., after the fall of the Roman Empire. They were our biggest seller for a good two hundred years. Our clients wanted to come back, but not until things settled down. Hence the 'term' in the policy. By the 14th Century Renaissance, we thought they'd become outdated. Then the Spanish Inquisition came along and bolstered sales for a good fifty years. Things have quieted down with occasional spikes since then. The term policy is perfect for those who wish to wait until the next Cultural Revolution or major technological innovation. Imagine coming back when you can fly."

"I fear the advances of the world have dulled rather than sharpened us spiritually."

"Of course." Reg forged ahead, barely digesting the comment. "I'm sure there are as many reasons as there are people. But, I digress." He reached into his desk and pulled out two folders. He placed a form on top of the folders and extracted a pen from inside his jacket.

"I'll need to add some basic information to the form you forwarded to my secretary. Hmmm, let's see." He scanned the sheet, mumbling various bits of information as he read. "Name, birthplace, employment, cause of death. You were quite young when you died."

"Yes. Longevity was never an option back then."

"Such a pity. Reincarnation is quite the rage for the early thirties age group, though it's bad for business. I think it's a passing phase. Remember nuclear energy?"

"Who could forget it? And reincarnation isn't all its cracked up to be."

"You know, just last month I had three Hindus and two Buddhists who signed up due to a fear of reincarnation. Who would have guessed it? Kind of against everything they were supposed to stand for."

"We often start out believing in something pure. It's others that dilute and pollute it."

Reg squinted for a few seconds longer than could be considered prudent. "Yes, well, as long as you're sure about leaving earth-bound desires behind, we can proceed." He handed over the piece of paper. "Scan all of the personal information to make sure there are no errors or omissions."

He took the sheet and glanced over it. "It all seems fine."

"Perfect." Reg pulled a sheet out from the top folder and handed it across the desk. "These are the actuarial tables for a man of your death. Now, should you want to remain dead for fifty years, the premium would be in that far column. One hundred years, two hundred, and so on. Our clients purchase piece of mind by knowing they won't be bothered for generations to come."

"It won't matter what's to come. I'm interested in complete coverage, if we could just cut to the chase."

"Very well." He calmly dispensed with the term rates and pulled a sheet from the second folder. "These are our most economical packages."

The man scanned the sheet without picking it up.

Reg sat forward and clasped his hands together with his elbows planted on the desk. "I had you pegged for a full timer. Life just didn't agree with you, eh?"

"Yes and no." He looked at his scarred hands and grimaced. There was so much he accomplished, yet so much left undone. "This wasn't an easy decision for me. I've had offers to come back, but I just don't have the stomach for it."

"I can see you waited quite a long time to visit our offices."

"This is not a decision I am taking lightly."

Reg gave a pert nod of agreement. "After enough time goes by, many people realize they don't want to be alive. All of the stress and complications of living can wear a man down. Death is not only natural, it can be quite relieving. We often accomplish more in our eternal sleep. Plus, you never know how you're going to fit in should you come back to life."

"That's not what bothers me about coming back. The world of men has changed so much since my day. I don't know that I'd even be accepted."

Reg sat back in his chair. "I always respect a man who knows his limitations." Without looking down he selected a piece of paper from the second folder and handed it across the desk. "This is an iron-clad death insurance policy with our famous 3-D clause. We assure you remain dead, departed, deceased.

"Sounds like what I'm after."

"We guarantee against reincarnation, voodoo, rifts in time, spiritual awakenings, and alien interference. We even have a codicil that addresses soul switching, which became so popular in the 1960s."

"What about third party situations?"

Reg's smile was for himself and not his client. "We wrote the book on supernatural visitation. Rest assured you will not end up a ghost rattling around in someone's attic. As for possession or manifestation, a thousand angels, demons, or mediums won't lay an ethereal finger on you. Resting in peace has never been so easy."

"Are there any exclusions?"

"Exclusions?" Reg waved his hand to push aside the thought. "You'd be hard pressed to find a viable one. There is an extra charge to include Natural Selection and Scientific Discovery, but I tend to steer my clients away from those. It's not really worth it and in all of my years, I have yet to see a client who utilized those benefits."

106

"And that's all of the exclusions?"

"Of course, there is the Act of God exclusion, but I don't know anyone who could honestly promise that. You'll find quite a few who will sell that at an exorbitant price, but I can bet you they are fly-by-decade companies you won't see around in the next millennium or two."

"Hmmmm…"

"So," Reg said with enthusiasm, "shall we start the paperwork and get you going?"

"Well, I appreciate your time and information, but I think I'll pass." He stood up to leave.

Reg rose halfway out of his chair, the first non-fluid movement he'd made the entire interview. "You should also consider our Enlightenment Package, a special bonus that I'll offer at cost if you go with a full Death Insurance policy."

"No, thanks. I'll just continue to take my chances."

"'Chance' is a dirty word around here. You won't find a better Everlasting Death product. That I can promise you."

"I don't doubt it."

"And if it's the Act of God exclusion that's causing you consternation, those odds are so astronomical as to be deemed miraculous."

"That's so true." The man looked out the window in the void. "Miracles aren't always a good thing."

Reg had been selling long enough to know when to let one go. Defeat had never been to his taste, but it was bad business to either harass a potential client or berate him. Future business depended on diplomacy. According to his statistics, those that initially declined came back 27.6 percent of the time. He stood and offered his hand with his fifty-dollar smile back in place.

"Do you mind if I ask why you really came here?"

His shoulders sagged as he turned to face Reg. "Peace of mind, I suppose. Searching for something that perhaps doesn't exist for me."

Reg nodded with a slightly pained look that might have passed for empathy on anyone else. "I wish you the best in your lifeless endeavors. Death isn't for everyone, but if you ever have a need for me, I'll be right here."

"Thanks." He shook Reg's hand and tried to raise a smile. It had been a long time since one had crept upon his face of its own accord. He knew coming here was a long shot, but so were most of the best things in death.

After the man left, Reg sat back down and put the folders and materials back in his drawer, leaving out the client information sheet. He scanned it over and allowed himself a satisfied smile. He'd heard about this guy. Peers told stories at office parties about how he tried this every eighty or so years. Now he had his own story to tell the others. If only word of His desire to never come back could be conveyed to followers on both sides of the void; what a major boon to the death insurance industry.

Slow Death

"I got the perfect crime, Latrell. Big bucks and big yucks, dude." Berry spit his chewing tobacco on the floor.

"I told ya, man, I'm keepin' it cool."

"You pussy-whipped, boy?" Berry looked at me as if I was one of them college boys he liked to bust up. One time I saw him punch a kid that called him an asshole in front of his drinking buddies. The guy's eye looked like a black egg with the yoke broken when they pulled Berry off of the dude.

"Maylene an' me. We got a good thing. That's all. Don't want to mess it up."

It was a hot July night at the Laughing Lounge, a place that hadn't been funny for about twenty years. No large screen TVs blaring out sports or karaoke nights. Happy hour? You'd be lucky just to get a few minutes. No amount of ammonia could cover the constant smell like dirty gym socks soaked in stale beer. The ceiling fan above our heads didn't really move any air; it always looked like it could barely muster the energy to keep spinning. 'Papa Was A Rolling Stone' was playing on the juke

"You got that muskrat love, like that song?" He raised his Lone Star bottle and gulped down a third of it. "More rat than musk, I bet. What, you both livin' in that piece a'shit trailer of yours?" He spit more chew on the floor.

"Lay off." I stared at my whiskey. The eight months Maylene and me had been together were the best of my life.

"Man, I need someone to help me with this job. It's a cinch."

"They always cinches until you get caught."

"I don't get caught. You see any stripes on me, man?" For all of the things he'd done, it was a miracle he never took a big dive. Lots of juvie, but nothing in the big house.

"You ain't gonna let me drink in peace until I hear you out, are you?"

He spit on the floor again. Barely missed my boot. "We're gonna rip off all them rich fuckers that live up on the hill, man."

"I ain't a burglar, Berry."

"No, but you're a driver. And a mover. And that's what I need. Someone to help me carry stuff and drive a truck."

"I don't know, man." I added my spent cig butt to the collection in the ashtray and fingered one of the many initials carved in the bar.

"I know this guy works for a security company." He leaned in and lowered his voice. "Installs systems in them big houses."

"Sounds sweet, but…"

"Goddamn, Latrell, my Daddy always told me there ain't no guarantees in life and even less in death, so raise hell before it rises up to get you first."

"I promised Maylene I'm through with that shit. After what happened to Ren."

Maylene's younger brother–Renfeld to those that named him and Ren to those that knew him–died last January.

"Ren fucked up. So did you. Remember that."

How could I ever forget?

*   *   *

Most of the security systems were door and motion sensor jobs with a keypad somewhere in the house to arm and disarm the system. Two modes. The HOME mode is just for the doors when the people are asleep. The AWAY mode added the motion sensor in the main rooms. If the alarm tripped, the cops came running because of the silent alarm wired through the phone lines to the station.

A lot of those fat cats, they kept fuckin' up. Some mornings they'd open the front door to get the newspaper and forget to punch in the code. Or they'd trip the alarm after a day trip by not remembering to disarm when they got back. This happened a lot with newly installed systems. The security company fined the clients a hundred bucks if they received two false alarms. After the third false alarm, the cops labeled the address as "repeat false trips—do not respond." Which meant they wouldn't cruise by or check out the place when the alarm went off.

Berry's man inside let us know what addresses were in the probation mode as well as those switched into the ARMED status for more than a day. We'd stake the place out, make sure the residents were away, and waltz right up with a Ryder van and rip them off in broad daylight. If any nosey neighbor asked what we were doing, we told'em we were making a delivery to Mr. So-and-so or picking up stuff the family wanted moved. Since Berry's man gave us the resident's vitals, we had all the right answers to any questions that might come up.

We only took the sure things. Cash, stereo equipment, TV's, jewelry–we made a killing. I was working nights at the lumberyard, so sneaking away during the day when I was supposed to be asleep was easy. Maylene never knew nothing about it, since she worked at the bank as a teller till four.

It was good being able to buy her the things she wanted. A new pair of shoes, tickets to the stock car races, or that Johnny Cash box set. We were livin' the high life. Even bought a round for everyone one night at the Lounge. Life was good.

But like most of the best things, it couldn't last.

* * *

Three weeks ago we busted into this house on Pershing in one of those fancy neighborhoods where they buy art and keep pedigree dogs and cats as pets instead of the mongrels and alleys we call neighbors. The family was definitely gone, but we didn't know about the nanny living there. She wasn't around the two days we scoped out the place. When we busted in, there she was, sitting on the sofa watching TV.

She was Puerto Rican or something, a pretty little thing in her early twenties. She screamed when she saw us, but Berry got to her pretty quick. I couldn't believe the sound his hand made when it first struck her face.

Blood got all over the white leather couch. He never gave her time to plead. He just kept pounding her like a butcher with a tough slab of meat. The squishy sound his fist made every time he hit her face made me want to puke. But I couldn't move. Felt like I did when I was a kid riveted to the screen of some sick horror movie. She was dead long before he let her body slump to the hardwood floor.

"Don't worry about her," Berry said, a little out of breath and sweaty. "She probably don't have nothing worth anything anyway."

I just looked at the girl. My arms hung limp at my sides.

He looked around to get his bearings. "Don't just stand there, asshole. You take down here while I hit the upstairs."

My body was paralyzed and my brain was pounding in my head. I couldn't remember why I was here. All I wanted to do was slink away and hide.

"The fuck you lookin' at, douchebag? Get your ass in gear." The muscles in his jaw tensed and his eyes were two black holes. He took a step towards me with one bloody fist raised. "You want a taste of this?"

I wandered into the dining room and shoved some silver into a box. Upstairs I could hear Berry turning the place upside down. The buzzing in my ears made it hard to think. I could see my hands in front of me, notice my legs walking forward, but I couldn't feel anything. We were in and out in less than an hour, but it felt like a couple years to me. For the first time in my life, I wished I was back in jail. At least in there I felt safe.

Berry couldn't stop talking as we drove away from the house on Pershing. Something like happiness had him higher than a meth bender, but not the kind of happiness you could appreciate or share. Whether it was the murder or the amount of stuff we stole, I couldn't say.

"Man, when I die, I'm goin' straight to hell." With his hand outside the window, he slapped the side of the car again and again. "Me an' the Devil. We'll just compare notes."

It'll be like they'd known each other for years.

*　　*　　*

When I got home that afternoon, I felt like something had crawled inside my skin and was eating me up from the inside. A hot shower couldn't wash away the chills. I curled up in bed and tried to force myself to sleep. That girl's face all mushed up and bloody kept looking at me. I must have passed out, because the next thing I knew it was dark and Maylene was next to me.

"You're cold, baby," she said. "You sick or something?"

My eyes cracked open. I didn't answer her. I couldn't.

"Ain't you going to work or nothing tonight?"

I looked at the clock. It was nearly midnight, which meant I had missed work and would probably get fired. It didn't seem to matter. The warmth of her body next to mine almost made me cry. I closed my eyes and tried to keep her out of my dreams. I didn't want to contaminate her.

Later that night I lay awake staring at the ceiling. Our trailer leaned a little to the left, so she was scrunched up on my side.

"Maylene?"

"Yeah," she said groggily.

"What do you think happens to a person when they die?"

She rolled over a bit to look at me. "God takes'em," she said with a yawn. "He's got Ren right now. Probably got him fixin' Harleys."

Ren loved motorcycles. He lived to ride'em and fix'em. Last January his cycle hit a cop car. Never saw it comin'. DOA. Losing her younger brother tore Maylene up.

"Maylene?"

"Mmmmmmm?"

"What do you think is gonna happen to me when I die?"

"You ain't going to die, baby," she murmured. "He ain't so cruel as to take both of my men."

112

*   *   *

"We're blood brothers, now, dude," Berry said next time I saw him at the Lounge after that job on Pershing. "'Til death do us part."

"Berry, I can't do this anymore." I had the shakes. And it wasn't from the whiskey. I was already out of cigarettes. The Budweiser clock above the bar said four thirty. It'd been that time since we got there an hour before.

"Man, you don't got a choice in the matter." He spit a stream of tobacco juice on the floor.

I looked him straight in those wild eyes. "What's that supposed to mean?"

"It means we're in business as long as I say we're in business." For a second, I thought he was going to up and punch me.

"Get someone else to go along."

"Shit." He leaned back and smiled, folding his arms across his chest. But his eyes burned right through me. "You worried about the cops? Hell, they got nothin' on that spic we did last week."

The cops hadn't pinned the maid's murder on anyone yet. She was an illegal, so I figure they weren't too upset about letting that one slip through the cracks. I leaned over to whisper to him. "You didn't have to kill her, dude."

"There's a lot of things I don't have to do. That don't stop me. You hearin' me clear, Latrell?"

"I hear ya."

Constance sauntered by us without a glance and took her place behind the bar to serve a couple of black dudes. Her breasts always seemed to be at attention—not infantry; they were definitely the rank of general. Three star at least. She had a leather vest over her dark blue Harley Davidson T-shirt. Her chest made that eagle proud.

Berry took a slug of his beer. "It's that slut, Maylene, ain't it? Man, she'll slice them balls right off ya until you're nothin' but a pansy ass like her older brother Arlin." He spit onto the floor. "Bet she still talks about Ren, don't she? Think she'd like a little history lesson about the day her little brother died?"

"Fuck you, Berry." I began to heft myself up and away from him when a rock solid hand grabbed my wrist and shoved me back into the booth. I had just enough time to prepare myself for the concrete hammer that slammed into my face and sent me reeling.

113

"Stick around, Latrell." He took a gulp from his bottle of Lone Star. "You and me got some planning to do. Why don't I call your pet muskrat and tell her you're gonna be late tonight?"

Violence gave Berry more of a hard-on than a two hundred dollar hooker. In fact, he liked to mix the two. I should have just picked my sorry ass off the floor and walked away from that booth. But I knew if I quit, he'd go after Maylene and tell her about what happened the night her brother died. And how I was to blame.

We did two more jobs over next couple of weeks. Any time I even hinted at trying to get out, Berry would leave me some sick warning. I woke up one afternoon and found a broken stereo receiver with a picture of Ren shoved in the works sittin' on the front steps of the trailer. Thank God Maylene didn't see it. It was the picture from Ren's obituary in the paper the day after he got killed. Another time, a Help Wanted ad from the place where Ren used to work was taped on the trailer door with a sticky note that read, 'Latrell, why'd you bust up my Harley?' and it was signed 'Ren.'

That's when I decided I had to break up with Maylene and move out. I told her she could stay in the trailer so she didn't have to live with the girls from the beauty salon again. She cried and wailed and told me she didn't understand. I couldn't begin to tell her. I just said it was for her own good. It tore me up inside, but I had to do it to protect her from Berry.

*   *   *

With no place to go I ended up spending most of my time at the Lounge. Wally, the owner, let me sleep in the shack out back of the place. There weren't no electricity or water, just four walls. It was pretty hot at night, the humidity making' me sweat like a junkie. The rats got pretty noisy, and I couldn't keep any food around. I got used to the smell of piss. At least I could take a hobo shower in the bar's bathroom.

All week Maylene kept trying to find me. Whenever I seen her coming I'd hide in the dumpster behind the Mexican joint down the street. I'd wait thirty minutes and then come back into the bar. Constance, Wally's main squeeze and head bartender, wouldn't even look at me, and I had to pay for all of my drinks in advance. And the pours were always short.

"I thought you was more of a man than that," Constance said without looking at me as she measured up a double shot of scotch for Cletus. "Maylene's had it tough enough with Ren getting killed. Now you up and leave without even tellin' her what for but you let her stay in your trailer? It's bullshit."

"It's best this way."

"Oh, yeah? Best for who?"

"Her."

"You're full a'shit, Latrell. If Wally ran off without telling me where we stood, he'd have a permanent limp after I got through with him."

I took another hit off my cig.

"She deserves better." Constance looked at me like I was one of the rats that kept me awake at night in the alley.

I could swear the clock behind the bar had moved to four thirty-one. "I couldn't agree with you more."

*   *   *

In the beginning there were four of us—me, Ren, Drew and Berry. We'd go out at night, about twice a month. Hijack a truck full of shit and sell it to Berry's contact for about a quarter of what it was worth. Cigarettes, home appliances, office stuff, car parts. Lots of stereo equipment.

Drew would sit in a car waiting for a truck to pass that looked like it might be hauling something we could sell. He'd radio on the CB asking if anyone was near a certain mile marker. That's where Ren would put his motorcycle with flares all around it like he was in trouble. It was a two-lane highway with a good-sized shoulder, so it wasn't no big deal for the trucker to pull over and help him out. One out of every four stopped.

Once the truck was at the side of the road, Berry showed up. He'd usually tag the guy with a gun butt to get his attention. I'd pull our truck around after the driver was bound and gagged. By this time, Drew would have caught up to us to help cross-load the merchandise into the truck. We were pretty slick. We changed our location all the time so the cops or the truckers wouldn't get hip to any pattern. After a couple of years, it went like clockwork. But we pushed our luck a little too far last January.

We were loading some stereo equipment when we heard the cops coming. Drew took off in the car. Ain't seen him since that night, and I always wondered if Berry tracked him down and killed him. Berry and me were in the truck and Ren was on his Harley. Ren was trailing because he could go much faster than us and figured he could throw them off our tail. I didn't see the black and white pull out in front of me.

That cop car was comin' straight at me. I swerved and somehow missed him. Ren never saw'em, never had a chance. The black and white hit him head on. I still hear the crash in my nightmares. That sound of rubber screeching on the pavement. The scream of crunching metal and shattering glass. The sound of the black and white flipping over and rolling after it hit Ren. The crash was so bad the cops let us get away so they could help their own. I think one of'em got hurt pretty bad.

We never even looked back.

115

Maylene and me had been going together for a couple of months by then. She didn't know her little brother died doing a job with us. And that we left him, all splattered on the pavement. Only Berry and I knew the truth. If I hadn't of swerved, it never would've happened.

*   *   *

Last Tuesday Maylene caught up to me out back of the Lounge. I awoke with a three-day stubble and a hangover like a sledgehammer cracking concrete in my head. My stomach was empty and I reeked of sweat. The stench of a gin vomit hovered from nearby. My lungs felt like a blowtorch every time I breathed and I could swear something had crawled inside my mouth and died. None of this hurt worse than looking up into her sad, longing eyes that dripped a tear on my cheek.

"What did I do to you?" Her voice was the definition of pain. "Why are you running away from me?"

"Maylene..."

"I just want to know..."

"Maylene..." I closed my eyes, but I still saw her face. The hurt. The confusion. It made me feel even sicker.

"I can't wait for you," she said, her voice cracking. "Not when you act like this. I don't know what's happened to us." She began to sniff and cry some more. "What's happened to us?"

Much as it hurt, I opened my eyes. I owed her that. "I can't explain it. I just can't. It's not you. It's me. It's always me." I rolled away to keep from breaking down.

"I though we were 'us'."

I wouldn't look at her.

"I don't understand," she whispered. I heard the sound of her walking away from me. "I don't understand." She kept repeating it. Her voice faded. My angel floated away.

I didn't open my eyes for another five minutes. The back door opened and I heard the clatter of garbage. I cracked my lids open just as Constance dumped a full bag of trash over my face.

*   *   *

Berry approached me in the Lounge two days later with a grin wider than the state of Texas.

"Got us a good one, dude. We strike tomorrow."

I was wallowing in self-pity. If I drank enough, maybe I could climb into the glass and be washed clean when Constance rinsed out the filth.

116

"Big score, man. Might even take me a vacation after this one. Got me a new squeeze."

I wasn't paying attention. Berry was always bragging about some chick he was screwing. Half the time I figured her name was Rosie.

"Get us a couple of drinks, Latrell, and I'll give you the lowdown."

I got up like a zombie and headed to the bar. Constance ignored me for a couple of minutes before grudgingly coming over. She didn't say anything. Just stood there with her hands on her hips staring' at the lost cause.

"Whiskey and a Lone Star," I said.

She didn't budge. Just stared right through me. After about twenty more seconds, she shook her head back and forth and walked away. Wally came over in another minute and laid down my drinks. I paid and retreated to the table where Berry sat.

"You'll make enough off a this score to buy you a friend," Berry said. "At least for a couple a days." He chuckled and looked over at the bar.

I eased back into the booth. My forehead found my palms as I leaned forward to gaze into the glass of brown liquor.

He hooked one finger over his bottle and leaned closer to me. "3540 Crescent View."

My head rose with recognition. "You said Crescent View?"

His eyes glistened and that sick smile of his mocked me.

"But that's—"

"Good. You'll know the layout."

"Goddamn it, Berry. Not there. I won't do it."

He grabbed my collar to pull my ear to his lips. "You'll do it. Or I'll tell her."

"We ain't together no more," I pleaded. "It won't mean nothing."

"It will to her."

"You son of a bitch." The fists I made under the table would never meet his face.

He pounded down his beer and stood up. "Goddamn right!"

I stood up slowly. "You're sure Arlin won't be there?"

"Of course, hombre. I got my own inside information on this one." He made a couple of humping gestures. "If you know what I mean."

My hands shot out to grab his shirt to throw him to the ground. But I was too drunk and weak to be any match for him. He deflected my assault and shoved me back into the booth. Then he placed both hands against the wooden bench and bent over me.

"A woman like Maylene needs a man to console her in her grief," he said with a smirk. "I'm good for at least three consolings a night. No wonder you was tired all of the time."

117

My whole body tingled. I wanted to hit him on the mouth, but I knew I'd wake up in the alley if I even tried.

"See you tomorrow night. Six o'clock." He straightened up and looked down on me. "I'll give Maylene your best."

I was trembling with hate and loathing. For him and myself. He turned around after a few steps to deliver a parting shot.

"On second thought, I'll give her *my* best."

* * *

Friday was a blur. Darkest day I could remember. Everything I tried to eat came back out. Tremors made it tough to even take a piss. And I was sober.

What was I supposed to do? Call the police and send myself up the river for years? Berry would figure some way to put it all on me, even the maid's murder. I'd be stuck inside while he stole Maylene. Even if I got off, he'd tell her about how I was responsible for Ren's death. I loved her. I couldn't let him hurt her like that. I wouldn't be able to live with the look in her eyes if she ever found out.

I sat in the Lounge staring into space and drinking Dr. Peppers to stay awake.

"You pathetic piece of shit."

I wasn't sure who said it. Could've been me. I glanced up to see Constance looking at me with her arms crossed over her massive chest.

"Tell me something I don't know," I said.

"I don't get you, Latrell. I just don't get you."

"Consider yourself lucky."

"You know Maylene's taken up with Berry."

"Yeah." I reached inside my pocket for a cigarette. The pack was empty.

"He's a worse piece of work than you."

"I know."

Constance shook her head again, like my mother used to do whenever I did something really stupid. "And all you can do is sit there and hide in a bottle."

"It's only Dr. Pepper," I said, trying to be funny. "Besides, finding me inside a bottle is a lot easier than outside of one."

"Pretty soon, no one's gonna try."

"Pretty soon," I said.

"He beat the shit out of her."

Her words cut through the cloud in my mind. "What?"

118

"This morning," she said. "Your friend Berry beat the shit out of her."

"He's not my friend."

"Whatever the fuck he is," she shouted. "The one thing I liked about you was the way you took care of her."

"What the hell can I do?" I'm sure I looked as helpless as I felt.

"What the hell *can* you do, Latrell?" She let out an exasperated breath. "That's the big question."

*   *   *

Four hours later we pulled up to 3540 Crescent View. Maylene's brother Arlin's house. Arlin made a shitload of greenbacks on the dot-com market. Got out before the bottom fell. If he was out of town, she might be house sitting. I had to figure a way to protect her. We saw the light on inside, but we figured it was one of those automatic jobs designed to fool burglars like us. As soon as we walked into the house, I knew someone was going to die.

"What the fuck are *you* doing here?" Berry's face was a mixture of surprise and molten anger when we saw Arlin standing there with a glass of wine in his hand.

Whereas you could see the resemblance with Ren and Maylene, you had to wonder if Arlin came from the same gene pool. He looked liked one of them sniveling little bookkeepers you always see in the gangster movies. He stood there gaping at us with a pissed look on his face.

"Look Latrell," Arlin said. "I don't know what you think you're doing, but–"

Berry slugged him in the jaw. Hit him so hard Arlin's feet went off the ground about three inches. The wine sprayed all over the carpeted floor, red stains that I knew wouldn't be the evening's last. I just stood there, unable to stop it.

Arlin was sprawled out on the floor. He rolled over and looked up, leaning on one elbow while his other hand massaged his jaw. Blood spilled out of both sides of his mouth. His eyes showed fear.

I looked over at Berry, his face twisted in a snarl. Arlin must have recognized the look, because he started to crawl in the opposite direction. After a few feet, Arlin got to his knees and made an effort to get up.

Berry was on him. A steel-toed boot to the face leveled Arlin. I heard something that sounded like bone crunching. He kicked Arlin three more times in the stomach.

"Goddamn it, Berry! You're gonna kill him!"

119

"Shut the fuck up, Latrell," he screamed as he stood over Arlin. "What the fuck are you doing here, you douchebag? Your sister said you was supposed to be at some convention this weekend. You wasn't supposed to be here!"

Arlin covered his head with both of his hands, so I couldn't see his face. His voice was barely audible. "Cancelled," he said between pained breaths. "Going next weekend instead."

"You ain't goin' anywhere instead," Berry said. He had his foot pressed on Arlin's neck.

"Take what you want." Arlin could barely get the words out. "Just don't hurt me anymore."

Berry took his foot off Arlin and kicked him again. A choked grunt escaped from the trembling body on the floor.

"That fuckin' bitch," Berry said. "Why didn't she tell me you was stayin'?"

"Goddamn it, Berry," I said, "how the hell is Maylene—"

"I thought I told you to shut up, Latrell."

Berry walked around so the heap that was Arlin was between us. He reached behind him. When his hand resurfaced it was holding a gun. He pointed the muzzle at Arlin's head.

Arlin must have sensed it. Or maybe he just smelled death in the air. His voice quivered, "Please. Don't. Please."

I looked down at Arlin for a second. The explosion of the gun didn't surprise me. The pain in my shoulder did. My legs buckled and I went to my knees. I looked up at Berry. The arm with the gun was pointing at me. My mouth felt dry, but I swallowed once, still staring with disbelief at my partner in crime.

Berry smiled, his teeth yellow from the chewing tobacco.

The second shot knocked me over. My face was on the floor. Blood flowed from somewhere on the side of my head. I could taste it. Felt the life draining out of me. My left arm got numb. I blinked a couple of times. Everything was getting blurry, halos over fuzzy shapes. The last thing I heard was Berry's voice.

"I'm gonna take care of that fucking bitch."

* * *

I woke up.
Where was I?
I licked my lips. I could still feel.
I blinked once. Carpeting. Blue. I could still see.

120

How about a fist? Could I make a fist? My right hand could do it, but my left didn't feel like it was there anymore.

My head pounded and my neck hurt, but that was a good sign. The right side of my skull was a mess of gooey flesh and warm blood. I didn't think you felt stuff like that when you were dead. I tried to push myself up from the floor. My left side was useless, so I rolled over to get some leverage. That's when I saw Arlin.

He wasn't moving. Just a heap about ten feet from me. I got to my knees and found a way over to him. His face was a pulpy mess. Sightless eyes lookin' up at the ceiling. I jiggled him once, but he didn't respond. I shook him real hard, and his arm fell from his waist to the floor. Berry's gun, at least the gun he shot me with, was in Arlin's dead hand.

Maylene. I was weak, but my mind was racing. Although dazed, I knew what I had to do. My life, or my death, depended on it. So did Maylene's.

Berry first shot must have lodged in my shoulder. It hurt like a bitch. Second shot took my right ear off, but didn't kill me. Not yet.

He'd left me there for dead. Now, I'm not a smart man, but I knew what he wanted the cops to think: I came over, robbed the place, and beat up Arlin. Beat him so bad he died. But Arlin shot me before he died. Yeah, Berry had it all worked out.

I prayed Maylene wasn't somewhere in the house. I searched upstairs and in the basement. Every corner I turned I said a little prayer that she wouldn't be laying in a pool of blood. Thank God I didn't find her.

Berry was out of control. What did he figure on doing about her? Even if he didn't kill her, how could she live with this? And how could I live or die knowing that she thought I was responsible for killing *both* of her brothers?

Arlin's car. I fished his keys out of a little glass bowl on a table by the front door. I don't know how I was able to drive to the trailer in my condition. Funny thing was all I could think of was how pissed Arlin would be about all of the blood on his carpet and upholstery. All of my cigarettes were wet with my blood and I couldn't get one lit. Something smelled like rotten meat, and I had a sinking feeling it came from me. Still, I was amped. I heard how when people go into shock, their bodies can do things they wouldn't normally be able to do. How much blood had I lost? How long had I been unconscious?

No cops stopped me on the way to my trailer where I hoped Maylene would be. Another break, I guess. Maybe things were starting to go my way. The place looked pretty desolate. I had no time for sneaking around so I pulled right up front. I didn't see the Ryder van or Berry's car anywhere. And Maylene didn't own a car. Lights were on inside.

"Maylene!" I called. No answer.

I must've looked a right mess, what with all of the blood. I didn't have my key to the trailer, but the door wasn't locked. I pushed it open.

No one inside. Real quiet. The place wasn't messed up no more than usual. Maybe Maylene was at one of her friends to heal from Berry's beating. Maybe he hadn't found her yet, and told her about Arlin. And Ren.

That's when I saw it. On the floor. On the wall. Still wet.

Tobacco spit.

I stumbled out of the trailer and back into Arlin's car. I guess I hadn't turned off the engine, because it was still running. I was about to shift into drive when I felt the unmistakable nose of a gun against my neck.

"Back from the dead?" I heard the sound of tobacco being spit onto the back seat.

"Never got there," I said.

"You going back there now," Berry said. His voice was cold and calm. "Drive."

"Where am I going?"

"Back to your grave, hoss. Back to Arlin's, where you was supposed to die. I hate doing things twice, but in your case, I'll make an exception.

I suddenly felt weaker than I'd ever been before. He had me. And he was enjoyin' it.

"You always did have bad timing to go with your bad luck, Latrell."

I didn't answer. We left the trailer park and drove along the two-lane road out to Arlin's. The wind had picked up and battled me for control of the car. I was getting dizzy concentrating on keeping between the white lines.

"Maylene's gonna be mighty upset," he said, goading me. "She's gonna need all *kinds* of sympathy."

I gritted my teeth against a pain inside worse than any of my wounds and accelerated the car without even thinking about it. Drove with my one good hand clenching the wheel. Blood pumped furiously through my veins. Felt it seeping out of my body and dripping down my side. I passed a concrete wall that rose up along the side of the road. Stared at it real hard. Swerved a little to miss an oncoming car.

"Shit, Latrell, you must be losin' it. Never seen you drive this bad."

We started to go up a hill. Towards Crescent View and Arlin's house. They built the nice places up a little higher. Guess the rich folks liked looking down on us other folks.

"Yep, sure is nice not having to split the take," he said from the back seat. "I never was too good at math, anyway."

122

The road veered around as we climbed the hill about a mile from Arlin's. Felt like I was gonna pass out. I had one last chance to make something happen, to make my life mean something.

Berry let out a holler and laughed. "Someday you'll have to tell me what you think of Hell, Latrell."

"I'll let you know when we get there."

I gunned the car and took a hard left where the road took a hard right. We slammed through the guardrail and hurtled over the side into the endless black of night.

Weightless. Like angels.

We plummeted to the quarry below. I closed my eyes. Berry's scream was the most beautiful music I ever heard. I thought of Maylene and smiled.

The Best Part About Dying–An Excerpt

Coming in 2015 is the first novel from Joel Reiff called "The Best Part About Dying." The book follows war veteran Parsons Prefontaine, who has been 'put out to pasture'. When his former comrade is assassinated at a political rally he realizes the deaths of others from his unit only months earlier is a plot to wipe away a piece of history by the US government. Born of violence and running away from a horrible past, he must stay one step ahead of the men seeking to kill him–the same men he once served.

Abel Dabney is bent on derailing the upcoming budget hearings that fund the covert operations he oversees. He will stop at nothing to protect himself and the country he believes he is serving, and the command that has stolen the years of his life.

Ensnared in the plot are a pair of covert ops that get in deeper mud than their boots can handle, a ghost-writing reporter looking for her big break, a forgotten war veteran out to make his final stand, a junkie who couldn't win if he was the only one playing the lottery, and a backwoods moonshiner trickier than a politician.

The country is about to be rolled like dice in a fixed game of craps. And something winning just isn't worth it.

None of this really happened. But…what if it did?

Chapter One

Parsons Prefontaine bent low to evade the sweeping light from creating a shadow of the man he used to be. Eight years ago the effigy of a tall, powerfully built soldier might have graced the wall. Instead of his shadow the light revealed black outlines of hospital beds across the wall. The images seemed to flicker and were gone, as if those still sleeping never existed. And to the outside world, they pretty much didn't. Had the searchlight known what it was looking for, perhaps it might have made a second pass to find him jimmying the door that would free him from what the Suits called the Sleeping Quarters. Hard to trust men with prefixes after their names that believed six years of school could teach more than a single day on a tour of duty. With a metallic click the lock relented and the door opened.

Until this morning time had never been his enemy. No one waited for him on the outside, though many had never forgotten him. It wasn't the confinement that finally pushed him over the edge. Nor the endless 'medications'. He could have stayed until he finally ran out of living. For the past eight years they'd shuttled him around the country to facilities hidden in small towns where the population couldn't afford to argue. Yesterday's transfer to this place in upstate New York changed everything. They wanted him dead.

The searchlight cycled every four hundred and forty seconds. Leland figured that out as soon as they arrived. Leland figured everything out. It passed by the hall windows leaving shadows of the iron bards at a skewed angle on the shiny tiled floor. He moved forward until he reached the next door. This he opened and walked into what the Suits referred to as the Community Room. The inmates spent most of their waking hours reading innocuous books, watching television shows to numb the mind, or playing various games of skill that only slowed their reactions rather than enhanced them. These places were all the same, at least in his eight years experience. Ping-Pong was the closest he got to maintain his uncanny hand-to-eye coordination. Nothing even remotely close to the precision of shooting a gun. The computers they were allowed to access were virtually useless; anything deemed 'controversial' was forbidden and conveniently locked from view. Majestic pictures of nature with motivational slogans ('Persistence: Challenges are what make life interesting; overcoming them is what makes life meaningful.') covered the walls. And always the air fresheners. Had to cover the smell of treason with pine or sandalwood.

A sound of a crunching rubber footfall behind him froze his progress. That old friendly adrenaline rush kicked in. He turned slowly and looked back down the hall he'd come down. The door to the sleeping quarters was still open. Had he closed it or was someone following him? After staring for a few seconds he wrote off the noise to another inmate having a nightmare.

He crossed through the Community Room, every fiber on red alert. The door that led to the doctor offices was unlocked. As he'd already jacked up the security system earlier in the afternoon, he knew the motion sensors wouldn't be operative. Leland had figured that out, too. Still, he moved forward cautiously. Another noise from behind halted him. Squinting back into the Community Room he saw a bluish light from the moon through the far too few window. He couldn't kick the sense that someone was following him.

At the end of the hall, past all of the doctors' private consultation rooms, was the heavy iron door that separated Limbo from the world of the living. An 'Exit' sign above that door cast a soft red hue. If the main door to freedom proved insurmountable, he'd have to go to Plan 'B', which meant a claustrophobic trip through the sewage system. He'd smeared Vaseline on his nose just in case to mask the stench of shit and urine, like they used to do in Iraq whenever foraging through a strafed town reeking of death.

The searchlight was due to sweep over him. He needed to stay on schedule.

Then he saw it. Light spilled underneath the last door on the left before the main exit. The Pharmacy door. Whoever it was, inmate or doctor, there was a good possibility that this person would have to get dead. He crouched low, just in time to evade the seeking searchlight.

As he crawled on hands and knees he heard a shuffling of feet and the sound of pills rattling into a plastic container. Medication at these facilities wasn't by need or choice, but by design. The Pharmacy light went out.

A shoe scuffed behind the door.

He readied himself for incapacitation rather than lethal attack.

The door cracked open slightly, a hand on the inside knob the only body part visible. Time dripped by. The room's interior light turned back on and the hand fell away from the knob, leaving both the door and Parsons waiting for a conclusion.

More shuffling of feet. The sole leather, not rubber, meaning the person was male. The vain women usually wore heals while the frumpy opted for rubber-souled footwear. The orderlies sported Nikes or Reeboks. All soft bottoms. Only the doctors with their patented leather afforded by government money made the sound coming from the Pharmacy.

Placing himself at the blind side of the door, he waited. The light clicked off and the door swung open.

Parsons, though rusty, moved as smoothly as the searchlight and had the man on the floor before either could think about it. The doctor lay with startled eyes and a muscular hand clamped over his mouth.

"You know what happens if I remove my hand and you make any sound?" Parsons asked.

The doctor's eyelids moved up and down. Parsons sensed the fear.

"All right." He slowly withdrew his hand but maintained a position of advantage with his body smothering the doctor's. "Doctor...Gaskins, is it?"

He fished into the man's coat and pulled out three vials and inspected the pills inside. All were generic, but the size and shapes made them easy to identify. Oxycodone, diazepam and ketamine. Psychedelics they'd used on him in the past. He shook the vials like mini-maracas. Without any facial reaction he shoved the pills back into the man's pocket. "Get up," he said as he rolled off Gaskins.

Gaskins hesitated.

He gave him a solid nudge with his foot. "Up. Now."

Gaskins got up and brushed at his coat a couple of times with shaky hands. "Is it Parsons, or...?

A push forward nearly made Gaskins fall flat on his face.

The doctor turned, his eyes squinting a question. "You don't have to do this..."

He fished a folded newspaper sheet from the pocket of his hooded sweatshirt and passed it to the doctor. It was the front page of *USA Today*.

In the dim red light from the emergency exit Dr. Gaskins focused on the newspaper. It was from three days ago, February 20, 2013. The centered picture was some Senator and another man. The headline shouted 'Aide Killed By Sniper.' "I don't understand. Is there something about this article...?"

Parsons' voice rose above the calm whisper he'd maintained until now. "He hasn't drawn a line in the sand; he's taken away the entire beach." He pointed at the newspaper. "It's murder. Plain and simple."

"What can one man do...?"

"They're about to find out." A snap from behind them accosted his ears, like an inmate stepping on a floor tile not quite glued all the way down. He whipped around. Still nothing. Agitation showed on his brow, in his voice. "Open that door, unless you want a permanent limp."

Doctor Gaskins knew that was no idle threat. The file was very clear. The man was the definition of dangerous. Sure, he'd been out of the field for nearly eight years. But, if he said he would break your neck, consider it as good as broken. He turned to the heavy door with the small, wired window around head height. "Think about what you're about to do. Think about Leland."

"This is the last time I'll ask. Open it."

Gaskins stooped over the keypad and stared at the screen. He typed in his personal code. After a mechanical buzzing sound he placed a finger on the pad and allowed the machine to read his print. A click reverberated down the hall. As soon as the door swung open he felt his body shoved heavily through the entrance.

"Timer." Parsons pulled the door shut behind them. "You think I didn't know about that?"

"Can't blame me for trying," Gaskins said.

"Yes, I can."

"How did you figure to get past the retinal scan if you hadn't found me?"

"Retinal scan?"

"Shit…" Gaskins gripped the article Parsons had thrown at him and squeezed it so hard the black ink rubbed into his hand.

After they completed the retinal scan the only thing that separated them from the street was the innocuous waiting room. One would never think while sitting in the comfortable cloth chairs reading months old issues of *Sports Illustrated* or *Time* that behind the door they just came through were some of the nation's most notorious instigators. Some were killers; most were worst. Parsons defied categorization.

"Where will you go?" Gaskins asked.

"Really, Doctor?"

Gaskins cast his glance up at Parsons, who at 6'4" towered over him. "The world has changed a lot since you've been inside. Their attitude towards you, though, has not."

"But, my attitude towards them has."

The doctor walked over and unlatched the front door. After all of the security checkpoints and heavy iron doors they'd been through, this momentous final passage into the real world seemed anti-climactic.

Parsons crossed the threshold and breathed in his first free air of a cold winter's night. He turned to face Gaskins, a man he didn't hate. Which was saying a lot compared to his feelings about some of the doctors in these places. He peered behind the doctor, still unable to shake the feeling that someone else lurked just out of his sight.

"Are you going to kill me?" Try as he might, Gaskins couldn't prevent his voice from cracking.

"Turn around."

The doctor's legs weakened and nearly buckled. Heaves came in waves. His eyes closed like a coffin lid. Would it hurt? Would it happen instantaneously? He began to sob softly. He wished it was for his wife or his kids, but it was for himself. Shame. Would that be his last emotion in this world?

After countless seconds he opened his eyes. The security door across the room was open. Another inmate casually stood there. Duke Devereaux. A small, innocuous, compact man built like a piston. What little hair he had left was grey and wispy. His eyes looked soft, almost innocent, as if the atrocities he had seen had sapped all the emotion from him. The map of his face spoke of many roads that led to dead ends.

Duke moved towards the doctor. Slow, measured steps, but with purpose.

Gaskins breathed the air of the living. He turned around to stare out the front door. The manicured lawn was empty under a sky where stars blinked suspiciously through breaks in the clouds. The solitary hooded figure of Parsons Prefontaine had vanished. The Simple Valley Mental Hospital and Research Center sign glowed in the ravenous darkness that would not be satisfied by the rising sun of a new day for a good five hours. It would only be a matter of time before the cops showed up followed by the federal agents and even worse. His exhale revealed that something momentous had just been set in motion.

"Ends and beginnings don't always quite meet, and rarely recognize each other when they do," whispered Duke.

Gaskins began to turn around. "How did you...?"

The searchlight made another sweep across the newly breached facility. The circle of white light hesitated for only a moment before reversing its direction and stopping on two figures arrested in the entrance.

Alarms cranked up. Light flooded the entire compound as the once slumbering giant awoke with a migraine.

Gaskins closed his eyes and covered his ears.

Duke stood behind the doctor, so the searchlight didn't capture the ghost of a smile on his thin, cracked lips.

Soon he too would be unleashed in the world.

Chapter Two

Cadence 'Cady' Devereaux paused as she reached the front door of the Simple Valley Mental Hospital and Research Center. Men and women in black vinyl jackets scurried around like mice trying to locate a single piece of cheese. On a normal day the place could be best described as a yawn after a good night's sleep. Although she didn't notice any signs of break in or fire, everyone moved with urgency.

She walked up to the front desk where every other Saturday she casually signed her name and flashed an ID before being buzzed into the Maximum Security building. Jenn, the woman at the counter who normally read romance novels while noshing on salted almonds, sat bolt upright with her lips clamped together and hands clenched on her desk, a government-wage scarecrow warding off only the wimpiest of birds.

"What's going on?" Cady asked.

"Uh…I'm not at liberty to say." Jenn's eyes darted around the room to check for eavesdroppers.

"Somebody bust out?"

Jenn's laugh was forced. Nothing could be that unfunny. "Someone killed him."

Cady's smile turned southward. "Who? Who got killed?"

"Dr. Gaskins…" Jenn's body shivered and she sniffed hard to hold back the tears.

"Where's my Uncle? Is he okay?" She placed both hands on the desk and leaned forward. "How did it happen? Who killed Dr. Gaskins?"

"Ummm…" The girl looked like she might break down. "You should leave."

"Where is my uncle?"

Every few months her Uncle Duke would be incommunicado for periods of up to six weeks. No reason was ever given. She just figured his mental state required isolation or something of that nature. The only doctor who took any time to speak with her was Dr. Gaskins. He was an angular man who always flitted around like he was ten minutes late for something. Not that he explained Duke's condition or offered any positive or negative feedback. Simple Valley was a rug under which much was swept so that it always looked clean. At least Gaskins had sympathy. The rest of the doctors only had paychecks.

Each time visitation was cut off, she would still make the two-hour trip because they would never contact her as to his condition improving or deteriorating. The shortest spell lasted three weeks. When she next saw him, he looked and sounded as laid back as he had before the episode. Time didn't flow in a linear fashion in here. He'd be right in his chair conversing with her as if they hadn't missed a beat.

A murder at Simple Valley. A chill made its way through her body; she'd never known anyone who had been murdered. As a ghostwriter for some of the *New York Times'* most prolific authors, she often wrote about human atrocities, but always felt disconnected. She said a silent prayer for Dr. Gaskins, and a different one for her uncle.

She moved past the secretarial desk without another glance.

"You can't do that," Jenn said. Her words were as weak as the free coffee, though she made no attempt to thwart Cady.

The forbidding door that always slammed behind her with a whoosh of air and the sound of metal clicking was open, yet still not inviting. A man walked past in an expensive dark brown suit and a cell phone glued to his ear. Down the hall were more men in vinyl jackets and a few in suits of similar dark, mundane black. They stopped their conversation and tilted their heads in her direction as she moved past them. She could tell that half of them admired her looks and the other half her chutzpah. It was a combination she cultivated.

The general population area swarmed with more unfamiliar people. Everyone seemed to be speaking at someone instead of to them. Only a few of the regular inmates were out in circulation and each one had dour looking men flanking them. She made a beeline towards Room F. At the entrance stood two men in a military 'at ease' pose that looked anything but relaxing. They were both dressed in generic black suits. Their facial expressions had been replaced with servitude. If Uncle Duke was behind that door she needed to see him and make sure he was all right.

"Excuse me." She tried to move past them, but they didn't budge. Nor did they say anything, so she reached around one of them to grab the doorknob.

The agent winced and held his ground. "Can I help you, ma'am?"

"You can help yourself by moving out of my way."

"Sorry, ma'am," he said without moving.

She pushed him aside to grasp the knob. Confidence Man #2 moved in a trained way to intercept her.

"You can't go in, I'm afraid."

"What are you afraid of?"

"Ma'am?"

She leaned in towards him. "What are you afraid of?"

The second suited robot gazed at the first with a lack of comprehension.

131

"Why don't you two collaborate on an answer and get back to me." She tried to wiggle past them to open the door. A hand on her shoulder caused her to whip around. She came face-to-face with a man who looked like a male model for a hair ad.

"Whoa, it's illegal to strike a federal agent," he said rearing back in mock fear and a condescending smile that made her wish she had her mace handy. "And a very bad idea, Ms....?"

"How do you know I'm not a Mrs.?" Cady asked.

"No indent on your ring finger." He gave a goofy kind of shrug. "Plus, a mouth like that? Odds are you're single."

"Who the hell–?"

The male model looked around. "Someone escort her out. And get her digits. That is one train that might be worth catching."

One of the door agents spoke up. "Apparently, that's her uncle." He pointed to the door of Room F behind him.

"Really?" the model said.

"Who is this jackass?" she asked the agent she had earlier denigrated.

"Javier Zemper." He clicked his heels together and gave her a slight genuflect as introduction. "You may call me Mr. Zemper."

"You don't look like a 'Javier'," she said. He was tall, probably six-two or three. Dark black hair in a wave that dipped just above thick eyebrows. Thin, but with an athlete's look about him. Probably a former footballer who'd stayed a little too far past his two minute warning. Guys like that were always so...disposable. There are moments in a woman's life when you meet someone and just know the two of you will click. This was not one of those moments. "I'm Cadence Devereaux."

"Cadence. I bet you've got a sweet rhythm."

"Excuse me?"

He looked down at her cleavage, held his eyes there for an unprofessional moment, and then looked at her with a lascivious smirk. "You certainly dress for success."

"You're a pig."

"With a big badge, if you get my meaning." He reached into his jacket pocket and showed her his federal identity card.

"Are you in charge?"

He ignored her question. "You come storming in here and think you can bully your way past everyone with your Queen Bee attitude and expect the rest of the hive to run for cover. Just because these men are polite enough not to bitch slap a five foot nothing woman with a stripper's body and a Napoleon complex doesn't mean I have any compunction, not to mention legal justification to do so."

"Napoleon won many battles," Cady said.

132

"Yeah, but he lost the last war and ended up in exile."

Her heart was racing. What bugged her what that he was right; she *was* used to getting her way. Most men let their penises assess her without their heads getting any input. As a journalist, that quality often gained her entrance where she wasn't allowed.

"Why can't I see my uncle?"

"As you can probably glean from what's going on around you, we have a 'situation' here."

"Someone killed Dr. Gaskins."

He looked around, irritated. "Why don't we broadcast it to anyone passing by in a car? Yes, Dr. Gaskins. Did you know him?"

"He worked with my uncle. So, yes, I kind of knew him."

Zemper perked up. "Did your uncle get along with him?"

"If you're thinking he would have anything to do with hurting Dr. Gaskins, or anyone for that matter, you're crazy."

Zemper looked around the room. "In case you haven't realized where we are, crazy is something they specialize in. Seeing as your uncle is a lifer, I wouldn't put anything past him."

Cady noticed people in white jackets dusting tables and doorframes. A group of agents flowed in and out of the drug dispensary room. The seated inmates being interviewed all had a look of disinterest. A couple of them actually smirked at their interrogators.

"Why are you here?" he asked.

"I've been coming to see my uncle every other weekend for the past nine years." She'd been a regular since she turned eighteen and was allowed by her family as well as by law to make her own decisions. Most of which lacked the approval of both. "Every other Saturday."

"Don't you have a real life?"

"Are you interrogating me?"

He blinked a couple times and pulled back ever so slightly. "No. I'm asking you a question."

"With all due respect…" Her eyes held his like a bird's egg she didn't mind dropping. "I don't know who the hell you are. I've never seen you here before, and as far as I can tell, there's no reason for me to answer you. For all I know you got that badge out of a Cracker Jack box."

"What if I told you I was with the CIA?"

"What if I told you *I* was with the CIA?"

He threw up his hands and turned his back to her. "I've got no time for this." His whistle was more suitable to hailing a cab, but two men straight out of the academy hurried over to his bidding. "This one." He jerked his thumb at her. "Out."

The new agents each reached for an arm. Her first kick made a soft muffled sound as the target that cushioned her attack crumpled with a whimper that would manifest itself as a forty-eight hour hobble and slightly raised pitch. Her fist was only slightly off target as the second agent remembered in a flash of pain how much he hated his job.

Cady leapt into a stance somewhere between tai chi and the World Wrestling Federation, but was unsure of what to do next. The heavy pounding of her heart beat at her temples. She felt but never saw Zemper's hand dart out. Next thing she knew her body was paralyzed, the electricity shut off. The ground lifted up to greet her with a soft thud and she found herself looking into Zemper's amused eyes.

A second face came into her refocused field of vision. The woman was a good decade older than she, probably approaching forty with the zest of a thoroughbred winning a race. Taut cheekbones supported steel blue eyes that could cut diamonds. Short hair that looked stylish yet official formed a light brown perimeter around her face, each hair seemingly the same length as its brethren, all well behaved. Cady found herself enthralled by the woman, wondering how someone so striking could look so unhappy. She had the countenance of an executioner looking forward to overtime.

The woman looked down at Cady. "Was that really necessary?"

Cady opened her mouth to answer, but no words came out. Somehow, she'd forgotten how to talk. Zemper, who still had a finger pressed behind her ear, let go.

The world around Cady came back into focus. The two men she emasculated stood up, albeit a couple inches shorter in stature. As the realization hit that Zemper had applied some type of Vulcan death-grip on her so did her anger return. She rose to her feet, barely able to contain an avalanche of words that fought their way out of her brain. The woman must have sensed the onslaught, for she was able to staunch the amassing flow of expletives.

"You're thinking how can you sue us for laying a hand on you," the woman said. "After you cuss Agent Zemper out. You see, however, you made first contact. These two could sue you for battery."

Cady couldn't believe what she was hearing. "They touched me first."

The corners of the woman's mouth turned up a fraction in a smile that gives frowns a bad name. "I didn't see it that way." She turned with exaggerated emphasis to Zemper. "You?"

"She struck first." Zemper had lost his bravado in her presence.

Cady looked from smug face to smug face. Her eyes appealed to one of the two agents she had felled, but he jerked his head away. "What the hell is this? Who the hell are you people and what gives you the right to abuse citizens who have done nothing wrong?"

"So many questions. Are you writing a book?" asked the woman.

Cady leveled her hardest glance at the woman. "No, just an article for the *New York Times*."

The mention of the seminal newspaper wiped the smirk off of Zemper's face. The woman, however, wasn't impressed.

"You'll need my full name, then," she said. "It's Willamena Pantera." She spelled out both names with pride.

"The Panther," Zemper said with the kind of admiration that bespoke of both a partnership and her superiority.

"You're not a reporter for the *Times*," Pantera said. "Though you may work in some capacity for the paper. Which makes you an intruder and a liar."

"Actually, it makes her one Cadence Jasmine Devereaux," Zemper said, reading from a file on his iPad.

Pantera gave her the once-over, stopping every so briefly to grimace at the cleavage her shirt revealed.

"She's a journalist. University of Pennsylvania. Minor in accounting." Zemper looked up from the thin computer. "Weird combination." He resumed reading. "Worked in the accounting firm of Eisner Amper in New York while in college. After graduation, kicked around the city for a couple of years honing her journalistic endeavors. Credits in the *Village Voice* and *Street Scene*. Hired by the *New York Times* nearly five years ago." He looked up with a question in his eyes. "Doesn't say what you do there. Also, doesn't mention ever being published."

"What else?" Pantera flicked a speck off of her suit.

"Blah, blah, blah," Zemper read on. "No questionable affiliations. Single. Probably a lesbian."

"You think you're so good at reading between the lines…" Cady raised the middle three fingers of her hand at Zemper. "Read this."

"What do you do for the *Times*?" Pantera asked. "A paper I read cover to cover."

"I'm a ghost writer." Despite all her efforts, the tone was defensive. "When you first read about the occupation of Wall Street? The killing of bin Laden, or the altercation in Syria? Those were my words." She threw out a list of names she'd ghosted for that included a few Pulitzer winners.

Pantera nodded, duly impressed with the depth of her work. "Bet that's a lucrative but soul scorching gig." She turned to Zemper. "I get the anger issues now. She's tired of being the fairy godmother; she wants to be the belle of the ball." Then back to Cady, without any empathy in her tone. "It's tough on you, isn't it, Pumpkin? But, I don't really care. The only story

135

here will be the press conference in about an hour. You're welcome to wait for that. Outside."

She glared at the female cop and her assistant douchebag with the hundred dollar haircut and thousand dollar suit. "Is this the part where you guys tell me how you're here protecting my civil liberties and how I should be thankful for all that you do?"

"No, this is where we tell you to leave," Pantera said.

Zemper took a step toward her, though after witnessing what she did to the last men that touched her, he advanced with caution. "I bite back, just so you know."

"Obviously not house trained, though." Cady rubbed the shoulder that had hit the ground first.

"The door is right that way." He pointed for her edification.

"I'm not leaving." Cady folded her hands across her ample chest and planted her feet firmly apart. She figured she didn't have a leg to stand on, but that had never stopped her before. "Not until I see my Uncle."

"Can you believe this woman?" Zemper asked the ceiling.

"Either one of you touches me and I'll raise holy hell in the press. I'll make sure the cops hear about it. And if you're the cops, I'll make sure the Feds hear about. And if you're the Feds…"

"Keep going," Pantera said. "You'll get to us eventually."

"Treating people like this, it's no wonder no one cooperates with the law these days." Most people got worked up over rough or unfair treatment, went home and stewed about it, and then let the anger fade with ounces in a shot glass or beer mug. Not Cady Devereaux. This could be the start of an exposé on police brutality and abuse of the law they were paid to uphold. Perhaps the big story she'd been striving to cultivate so that she could get her own byline instead of polishing someone else's journalistic sterling silver.

"We have no need for your…cooperation." The last word came out like a bad taste Pantera couldn't wait to get out of her mouth.

The door to Room F opened. "But, you do need her." The voice was old and brittle, sounding of too many years of cigarettes and whiskey.

All heads turned to see the author of that voice, a small but compact old man. Brown age spots dotted his wrinkled skin. A 'U'-like scar on his forehead left the skin discolored. Wisps of fine white hair bathed in a bald sea. Under thick white brows were hawk-like eyes that darted from face to staring face as if trying to pick out which was the most important to peck. When his eyes fell upon Cady he looked almost content.

"And who might you be?" asked Zemper.

The old man flashed a tired grin. "Duke Devereaux. The man who just might help you locate Dr. Gaskins' killer—one Parsons Prefontaine."

We know who we are looking for," said Zemper. "We don't need some Ouija board slinging relic—no offense—wasting our time in locating him."

Duke's smile broadened with each word out of Zemper's mouth until he almost looked happy. "Who you are looking for is only one piece of a deeply intricate puzzle. Do you know 'what' you are looing for?"

"An escaped inmate. One capable of murder," said Pantera.

Duke turned slowly to regard her. "With those pieces you will never solve the puzzle. It's what you don't see that will be your undoing."

Zemper threw up his hands dramatically and began to pace the room again. "I hate people who speak like a combination of Shakespeare and a villain from *Batman* comics. Spit it out, old man."

"The man you are looking for are two men, both capable of destruction on a massive scale devoid of emotion." Duke folded his hands in his lap. "And both men are very pissed off."

"At whom?" asked Pantera.

"The entire United States government."

www.ingramcontent.com/pod-product-compliance
Lightning Source LLC
Chambersburg PA
CBHW060622130626
46555CB00002B/623